ALEXANDER'S BLOOD BRIDE

Vampires of London Book 1

LORELEI MOONE

CONTENTS

CHAPTER ONE

"I have amazing news!"

Cat looked up to find an excited looking Shelly standing in the doorway to their shared apartment.

"So do I," Cat responded with a wide grin on her face. The letter that had sparked her excitement lay in the center of the coffee table, just waiting to be shared with her best friend and roommate.

"Here," Shelly said, handing Cat yet another envelope. This one was different, heavy, made out of expensive looking paper.

"I've scored us an invite to the event of the year!" Shelly squealed and clapped her hands as Cat carefully opened the envelope to reveal a matching card with ornamental writing on it.

"What is it?" Cat held up the invitation to the light, noticing how the gold text shimmered luxuriously as she tilted it. The card stock itself seemed to have some texture and inherent glow as well. It was mesmerizing to look at, and almost made Cat forget about her own good news.

"This girl at work had a spare invite. Apparently this is an annual affair, been going for years now. But it's quite exclusive, not too many people know about it." Shelly's voice became more hushed as she continued to speak, like she was sharing a well-kept secret.

If there were so many printed invitations for it that Shelly got one off some random person who also worked at Superdrug, it couldn't be all that exclusive, surely!

Cat scrutinized her friend. Shelly was always the life of the party, wherever she went. Cat, on the other hand, was much more of a homebody. She didn't enjoy the club scene as much, no matter how hard Shelly had tried to convert her ever since they moved in together years ago.

It wasn't that she didn't like music, or cocktails, or even dancing. What she didn't enjoy was attracting attention to herself. Cat wasn't as popular or pretty as Shelly and for the most part, she was fine with that. She just didn't appreciate having her nose rubbed in it whenever they went out together.

"And it's fancy dress..." Cat noted.

"Yeah, obviously! What else is a Halloween party supposed to be?"

Urgh. Fancy dress was just an excuse for most people to dress up in as little as possible. None of what she'd heard so far had made Cat want to go to this thing.

And yet, the slight shimmer of the heavy card stock and the seductive curls of the golden writing continued to catch her eye. The invitation even *smelled* tempting; sweet, with a hint of pumpkin spice.

"Look, the best dressed guest will even win a prize!" Shelly leaned over and pointed at the relevant line. £1000 wasn't a small amount; no doubt Shelly would pull out all the stops in an attempt to win.

"Let me guess, you already have a costume picked out?" Cat said.

Shelly responded with a wide grin. Of course she did.

If not this party, she would have gone somewhere else on Halloween. She'd probably started thinking about her outfit months in advance. Shelly wasn't one to half-ass a costume party; she thrived on them.

"Anyway, so this seems right up your alley. What do you need me for?"

"Oh, come on! It's not every day you get a chance like this! And it'll be a hell of a lot more fun than sitting at home watching old movies all night!"

Cat made a face. "Wanna bet?"

"The card says *plus one*. Be a shame to waste it. Plus, after all the job applications you've sent out lately, you deserve to have a little fun." Shelly looked at Cat with big, pleading eyes. She could be so pushy at times.

Cat looked at the card again; every time she did, that little voice in her head screamed louder. *Stop being such a spoilsport and just agree already!* And indeed, ever since completing her degree in Art History just before the summer, Cat had been trying her best to get a job that would allow her to put her education to use. She'd been on the verge of giving up, because none of her applications had led anywhere... Until today.

Perhaps it was a sign. After she finally received good news today, what if this party was meant to be her chance to celebrate starting a new chapter in her life?

In any case, Shelly didn't seem in the mood to drop the topic. Cat could always tell when her roommate and best friend was going to dig her heels in.

She took a deep breath. *Just this once.* "Fine. Fine! Happy now?"

"You've made the right choice. You'll see."

Cat shrugged. *Bah. Fancy dress.* "I guess now I'll need an outfit too."

"Shopping spree!" Shelly clapped her hands in excitement. "On the way out, you can tell me all about your news too, okay?"

Cat leaned forward to grab her envelope off the table and handed it to Shelly. "Read it."

Shelly did as asked. "Oh my God! You've got a job?"

Cat nodded, her chest almost bursting with excitement. "Well, an internship, but it is paid, so that's basically like a job, isn't it?"

"I told you it would work out eventually. Come here, you! I'm so happy for you!"

Cat got up from the sofa and was immediately pounced on by Shelly, who gave her a big hug.

"Here's what we'll do. First we go sort out your outfit, and then I'm taking you out for a few drinks to celebrate. What do you say?" Shelly didn't wait for Cat's agreement, instead taking her hand and leading her out of the apartment so quickly, she barely managed to pick up her coat and handbag on the way.

——◆——

Cat smoothed the velvety fabric down herself as she checked out her reflection.

Not half bad.

Granted, the medieval style deep burgundy gown had been one of the very few choices in her size, and expensive to boot. But it fit Cat like a glove and accentuated her best features: her curves.

"I'm telling you, you look amazing," Shelly insisted, and rested her hand on top of Cat's shoulder.

Cat turned to face her friend and smiled. "I'll just pretend I'm meant to be an extra from Game of Thrones. That's still popular, right?"

Shelly grinned and nodded. "That's the spirit. Just give me a moment to fix my hair and we can go."

Cat watched Shelly as she fluffed up her blond curls, making sure not a single one was out of place, before pushing a flower wreath down on top of them.

Her costume was a sort of cross between stripper and fairy, with the most elaborately decorated net wings Cat had ever seen. The overall effect was impressive, if a little revealing. Of course, that was exactly how Shelly liked to dress when she went out. There was no way she'd end the night alone.

"You look great too," Cat said, as she ran her fingertips over the edge of the sparkly wings.

"They won't know what hit them when the two of us

arrive." Shelly giggled.

The doorbell rang, signaling the arrival of the cab they'd booked. You didn't turn up at a fancy party disheveled and windblown after braving the public transport and autumn rains, Shelly had insisted.

Cat took one final look in the mirror and off they went. She had no idea what to expect. The card, combined with the address at the bottom, had seemed quite fancy indeed. But if it was so special to be invited, how come the two of them had snagged a card? They weren't exactly part of London's high society.

Even the cabbie seemed surprised when Shelly told him the address. Cat imagined that it wasn't every day that two working class girls asked to be picked up from their tiny shared apartment in Shepherd's Bush and driven all the way to Kensington Palace Gardens, London's most expensive street. Luckily, the man didn't make a fuss about it.

As they pulled into the road, Cat finally did understand his reaction though. Just the size and scale of the first houses she saw were enough to take her breath away. Ever since moving to London a couple of years ago, she'd never visited this part of the city—why would she? Ordinarily she would have had no reason to.

"There it is." The cabbie pointed ahead at a beautiful Georgian villa.

As he pulled into the driveway, the ornately decorated iron gate opened by itself to let them in. The cab crawled up the immaculately kept gravel driveway and came to a halt in front of the house itself.

"Wow," Shelly said.

Cat just stared up at the impressive façade and blinked a couple of times, lost for words.

Was this really the place? She didn't belong here. They ought to turn back and forget about this whole party business.

"Come on!" Shelly urged and prodded Cat with her elbow. "Let's go!"

Cat took a deep breath and paid the driver before getting out of the car. She smoothed down her dress and did her best to stay balanced as she walked up the half dozen steps to the large double front door.

As soon as Shelly joined Cat in front of the entrance, the two doors swung open as if by magic, giving them the first glimpse of the party that was well underway inside. At least it was the right place.

Cat turned back one last time and caught a glimpse of their cab leaving. There was nowhere else to run.

Shelly took her by the arm and almost dragged her inside.

They were both speechless. They both stood there, looking up at the most beautiful carved wooden staircase Cat had ever seen. In the center of the ceiling up above was a giant crystal chandelier, its light refracting and dancing around on the walls and parquet floor below.

A waiter arrived seconds later, offering them a glass of

champagne.

Shelly emptied her glass immediately, but Cat wasn't much of a drinker. She sipped it slowly, and tried to take in as much as she could of the lush interior. This mansion didn't belong to some footballer, or other nouveau-riche celebrity. The place screamed old money.

As luxurious as it looked, it was tasteful.

Within minutes of their arrival, Shelly couldn't resist the pull of the festivities, and Cat found herself alone. She didn't mind. The champagne was lovely, refreshing with just a hint of citrus, and if Cat was left completely to her own devices, the decor alone would keep her entertained all evening.

Cat gazed at the staircase again. What wonders awaited up there? If she wasn't polite to a fault, she would have been tempted to check it out. She wouldn't, though. Not unless she was invited to.

Her eyes settled on a painting of a man on horseback that hung on the left hand wall closer to ground level. She squinted to get a better look; it seemed old, probably expensive just like everything else in here. But that wasn't what had attracted her gaze. The hunting scene looked just like the standard fare you found in country houses and palaces around the country, except the man was dressed completely in black.

She felt a chill pass down her spine as she focused on his face. His dark eyes gave the impression of being alive as he seemed to stare down at her. How handsome he was.

He would have had a striking presence back in the day with his sharp jawline, impossibly flawless skin, and dark medium length hair.

If she found nothing else of interest here—which was unlikely—this one painting could captivate her for hours. That was how lifelike it looked.

Cat had to admit Shelly had been right: she'd never been to a place or a party quite like this one before.

CHAPTER TWO

Alexander Broderick stood at the top of the curving stairwell in the center of his Kensington residence, surveying his domain. The party had started at eight sharp, with more guests arriving every few minutes.

His Halloween parties were an age old tradition, even if their grandeur and scale had evolved significantly since the early days. A hundred years ago, he'd been content inviting a few friends and acquaintances, all of them vampire like he was. Now, every year, the event had grown bigger and better, featuring new faces from all walks of life.

Eternity was a very long time to spend in isolation. He craved the change in routine, no matter how hard his maker had tried to discourage him from going overboard in the past. Of course, ever since Julius had taken over the Council leadership, he had other things on his mind than to monitor Alexander's social life.

Alexander thrived on the attention these parties afforded him. On a night such as tonight, he could step out of the shadows and into normality. Even if some guests noticed strange things around the house, they'd accept it as part of the magic of Halloween. It also helped that he kept the alcohol flowing generously throughout the night.

Tonight was the one night per year that the weird and

wonderful became acceptable.

He took a deep breath and closed his eyes. So many people. So many aromas.

His parties weren't an excuse to feed as such; no, he could do that any time. But the sheer variety of humankind at his feet was difficult to ignore.

Every vampire in attendance tonight would feel the same way. Alexander smiled as he imagined the depravity that would occur within these walls.

Sex, blood, and rock 'n' roll. Alexander couldn't suppress a chuckle.

They'd keep things clean enough, of course. Everyone here was keen to stretch the rules but not break them. They wouldn't take things so far as to attract suspicion.

They wouldn't kill.

Alexander himself would join in the festivities as well. But first and foremost, he enjoyed playing host. He was especially fond of striking up conversations with first-time guests. First he'd figure out how they'd come by an invitation, then he'd guide the conversation toward other topics that interested him.

He was a connoisseur of sorts; like some immersed themselves in fine wines, politics, or even sports, Alexander collected knowledge on the human psyche. *Zeitgeist,* as some people called it; he loved to learn about that special set of thoughts and ideas that made society tick. In gathering information about how people lived their fleeting lives, he sought to find meaning for his own.

As he slowly started to walk down the stairs, he focused on acting *normal*; that meant being a lot more clunky and obvious in his movements than his instincts dictated.

He was socializing, not stalking prey!

That was one of the first lessons he'd learned once he started inviting humans to his get-togethers. If you approached them in too stealthy a fashion, they easily got spooked.

Halfway down, his friend Michael nodded a greeting as he passed him by. The much younger vampire wasn't one to waste time; he'd already found himself two willing females to spend what he liked to call 'quality time.' Everyone had certain talents; seduction was his.

Alexander was about to continue down the steps when a presence caught him off guard. He wasn't sure what it was exactly. A quick scan around the room revealed that all the guests were quite busy entertaining themselves; nobody was looking in his direction.

He sprinted back up the stairs, faster than a human eye could see, and gazed back down to figure out what had affected him so.

The front door swung open and two women entered. One was quite ordinary, and he could hardly tell her apart from the two Michael had just led upstairs. The other, though...

A radiant sight of womanhood.

Her floor length gown was very different from the

skimpy outfits everyone else had chosen to wear. Blood red—which in itself would have been enough to entice even the most reclusive vampire among his company.

Raven hair halfway down her shoulder, which swayed with every step she took.

A face flawless, like that of a porcelain doll.

And curves. Her body exuded a richness that made every fiber in his body ache for her.

As different as they were, the two new guests couldn't have been a day older than 25, much younger than his usual choice of conversation partner.

He held on to the banister with both hands, then had to force himself to let go when the wood groaned under his tight grip. A lot could be forgiven on All Hallows' Eve, but destroying the furnishing with his super-human strength would raise a few eyebrows.

Alexander focused his hearing on the two women who still stood indecisively in the hall. One of his staff immediately approached them with a welcome drink.

"Thank you," the dark haired beauty said. *The voice of an angel.*

The blond didn't speak; instead, she just chugged the champagne and placed her empty glass back onto the waiter's tray. Alexander recognized her type. She gave the impression of a hunter among humans; she knew what she was after, and was scouting the place for the right mark.

Alexander stood frozen in place, waiting for the woman in the red gown to make a move.

The blonde had taken a few steps forward and spotted the dance floor in the reception room. She waved at her companion to join her, who refused.

"You go ahead. I'll hang back and get a feel for the place first," the medieval angel said, then took a small sip of champagne to make her point.

Alexander smiled and closed his eyes. Perhaps his senses were deceiving him tonight, but he could swear that he could catch her scent all the way up here.

A hungry vampire could smell his prey from nearly a mile away. But Alexander wasn't hungry.

At least not for nourishment.

From the moment she'd entered, the quality of the air seemed to have changed.

He knew he had to have her before anyone else. He would get to know this young woman, learn all he could about her. Take her to his chambers and bed her. He would taste her very essence. He had to. His instincts gave him no choice.

Before he opened his eyes, he knew she still stood in the same place; he could sense it. When he looked down at her, he noticed that it wasn't just him who had noticed her.

A half dozen sets of eyes had shifted in her direction.

Could they smell her too?

Alexander rushed down the stairs again, almost forgetting to follow the usual tricks to appear more human. So far so good: the other vampires had spotted her, but stayed back for now. He would reach her first. If her arrival had made this much of an impact, he would have to take it upon himself to ensure her safety here.

This was his house after all. His party.

He'd never been one to lose his tongue in company, but the closer he got to the woman, the more uncertain he grew. She wasn't just any other human to him; she was a whole lot more special than that.

"I hope you're enjoying yourself?" he said as he reached her side.

She looked up at him, her eyebrows pulled together in surprise. "Who, me?"

"Yes, Miss..."

"Uh... my name's Cat."

"Short for Catherine?" Alexander asked, mesmerized by her pale green eyes as she continued to look up at him.

She looked so vulnerable. He could hear her heartbeat, and the rush of her blood as it was pumped through her body. Being so near to her tested his patience like nothing ever had. If he'd been starving and faced with a first meal in weeks, he would have found it easier to walk away than he did now. There was something very different about this woman, though he had no idea what it was.

"I suppose, yes. Short for Catherine," she stammered.

He wasn't trying to hypnotize her, at least not on purpose. Was she under his control already?

How was that even possible?

"I said I hope you're enjoying yourself," he said, repeating his first question.

"Oh, yes." Catherine raised her glass and smiled briefly. "And what a beautiful house this is. I've never seen anything like it."

That gave Alexander his opening, a chance to get her away from all the hungry stares from every vampire in the room.

"Perhaps you'd like to see more of it?" he asked, smiling subtly to avoid exposing his sharp canines.

Catherine didn't answer straight away, instead continuing to stare at him. Hopefully, she wasn't actually hypnotized. Alexander was looking forward to having a natural conversation with this woman. Not a forced interrogation while she was under his influence.

"Don't tell me this is your place?" she asked at last.

Was she just nervous? Could that be?

Alexander winked at her in an attempt to break the tension and gain her trust. "Okay, I won't tell you that it is."

"Holy shit." Catherine immediately covered her mouth with her hand as she looked around the entrance hall again. "I'm sorry."

"You have nothing to be sorry about. My offer still stands by the way. If you want a tour..." Alexander said.

She looked into his eyes and there it was again, that strange feeling that had overcome him from the moment she'd entered his home. He had to have her, discover all there was to learn about her. Intellectually, physically, even spiritually, if that even made sense.

"I'm sorry, I just didn't expect to end up here chatting with the host of the party straightaway. Yes. I'd love a tour," Cat said while straightening her shoulders.

So she had just been nervous.

He wasn't sure why, but that pleased him. Probably because he'd been a little nervous at first too.

It was silly. He'd walked this earth for centuries and seduced plenty of beautiful ladies in his day. As delicious as this woman smelled, what did he have to be nervous about? He offered her his arm, which she reluctantly accepted. Her touch seemed to burn through his tuxedo right into his skin, almost painfully.

"We'll start with the downstairs," he said.

As Alexander led her past some of his immortal guests into the reception room, he felt their eyes on the two of them. There was no emotion as powerful to the senses as jealousy. Perhaps his nerves had been trying to tell him something. This party wasn't like every previous one. This time, he was playing with fire.

CHAPTER THREE

I'm such an idiot.

Cat straightened herself in an attempt to seem confident, even if she felt anything but. This handsome man—the actual host of the party and owner of this amazing house—had approached her and offered her a tour. And what had she done? Fumbled over her words and acted like a complete moron. Could it get any worse?

"I'd love a tour," Cat said and glanced at his face again.

Although he was wearing a mask covering the better part of his face, it was obvious that he was gorgeous. Those brooding, dark eyes... They alone spoke a million words.

And he was built too. Taller than her, with broad shoulders and a toned, athletic body which his three-piece suit could scarcely disguise.

He made Cat nervous, which was unusual. Cat wasn't the sort to get nervous around members of the opposite sex. Of course, she wasn't as outgoing as Shelly, but for most of her life, Cat had gotten on better with men than with women, platonically. Possibly that was a side effect of growing up with two older brothers...

Somehow though, this man was different. He intimidated her and made her feel out of her depth.

Was it because he was so handsome? Or so wealthy?

How shallow.

No, Cat couldn't accept that. There was something else about him which she couldn't quite put her finger on.

He guided her around the downstairs of the house. Through the reception and the dining room, as well as the very spacious kitchen. Cat couldn't be sure how the house normally looked; it had obviously been cleared out to accommodate tonight's party guests. She would have loved to see the normal layout and furnishing instead of this bare bones version.

"Would you like to see the upper floor now?" the man asked. There was a strange glint in his eye.

Cat glanced away shyly. Was that what had thrown her off? The way he looked at her? Nobody had ever looked at her like this.

"Sure, that would be great," she said.

He gestured at the stairs. "After you."

As she climbed up, she couldn't help but take another good look at that painting that had caught her eye earlier. It was even more stunning up close. Even though she could see the brush strokes in the landscape, the figure on horseback was still so lifelike. Like it was a photograph and not a painting at all. The only thing that gave it away were the fine cracks in the varnish, a clear sign that it was much older than anyone in attendance here today.

"Beautiful artwork," Cat whispered, barely loud enough to hear over the music coming from the reception room.

"Oh. Yes, this piece has been in the family a very long

time." The man smiled at her again. "If it's art you're interested in, I have some more items you might want to see."

Although she'd wanted to stop and admire that painting some more, her feet seemed to want nothing more than to carry her up the stairs. It was effortless, like she was floating.

"So this house has been in your family for a while then?" Cat asked, as she paused and held the banister with both hands at the top of the stairs. The view of the ongoing party down below, lit up by that magnificent chandelier, was something special. It made her feel powerful to be up here.

That was when she noticed a pair of red eyes burning into her from the foot of the stairs. The man, who looked to be in his mid-thirties, stood completely still as he stared at her. He didn't even blink once, which seemed unusual for someone who was obviously wearing contact lenses. An uneasy tension grew inside Cat's chest, forcing her to look away from the strange man to regain her composure.

Only then did she realize her host hadn't answered her question. And in fact, she didn't even know his name yet.

"You never introduced yourself," Cat remarked as she faced him.

He took his position next to her at the banister and looked down like she had only moments earlier. Would he notice the weirdo downstairs?

"Alexander Broderick the Third," he said. His voice

was low, like he was preoccupied with something else. So he *had* noticed.

That name, though. It was as grand as the house itself and she might have been way more skeptical of him had she not run into him here.

"Nice to meet you," she said and followed his line of sight down.

The strange man was no longer in view. What a relief.

When she turned to face Alexander again, she found that he was already looking at her with the subtlest of smiles on his lips. She couldn't help but reciprocate.

"How about I show you the master suite?" he suggested.

His proposal was forward, crossing the limits of propriety.

Cat frowned. She ought to change her mind about this whole house tour business and get back downstairs and try to enjoy the party. She really ought to... And yet, her feet refused to move.

"It's not what you think, I promise," Alexander added, raising both his hands in a defensive gesture. "There's this beautiful painting I'm sure you would appreciate."

Cat cocked her head. Nothing in his eyes suggested that he had any ill will toward her. And even if this beautiful man was indeed trying to seduce her, was she seriously about to reject him? Would it be so bad to just take a chance for once? To jump in the deep end and see where tonight would take her?

Cat took a deep breath and smiled through a fresh surge of nerves. "Okay, sure."

Alexander offered her his arm again, which she took as he led her away from the staircase and into an elegantly decorated hallway. A similar, though smaller crystal chandelier adorned its ceiling, and paintings lined the walls. There were more hunting scenes, some still lifes and portraits, though none captured Cat's imagination as much as that first painting along the staircase.

The further they went, the fainter the music became from the party below. Until one of the doors lining the hallway opened seemingly by itself, revealing not just a breathtaking array of period furniture, but also the painting Alexander must have referred to.

Cat let go of Alexander's arm and approached it. Expert brush strokes had created a completely realistic likeness of the house they found themselves in. It must have been painted in midsummer; the front drive and lawns were lined by a dazzling array of flowers which Cat didn't know the names of. She just knew they were beautiful.

"I love the light in this one," Alexander spoke behind her, his voice dreamy; he was obviously as enthralled by the painting as she was. "So realistic. A beautiful summer's day the likes of which I haven't seen in a very long time."

"You're right, the summers have been atrocious these past few years," Cat agreed. Still, she couldn't tear herself away from the image of the house.

It was perfect; blue skies reflected in the windows, just like a photograph. She leaned forward to get a better look and noticed the front doors were ajar and a figure waited just inside with its back turned. It made no sense of course, but as soon as she'd spotted it, she felt herself drawn to the house and wanted nothing more than to step inside.

Ridiculous. It's just a painting after all.

Cat turned and found that Alexander was already looking at her. He held two elegant long stemmed glasses in his hand.

"Champagne?"

Cat took a step back and scanned the room. Where had he got those from all of a sudden? Had this room already been prepped, just waiting for whoever he chose to bring up here?

She was about to protest when music started to play in the background. Something classical, she wasn't sure what it was.

Now where was the music coming from? She hadn't seen a stereo or even speakers anywhere. They'd look so out of place with all of this regency furniture that she was certain she would have noticed them on her way in.

Before she knew it, she'd accepted the champagne flute.

"To great art and great beauty," Alexander said and raised his glass for a toast.

She followed his example, even though her heart was

hammering in her throat now.

"To art," she mumbled.

What's going on here? None of this makes any sense. Was that first drink spiked?

Against better judgment, she took her first sip and felt her worries dissipate. So what if he was plying her with drinks. So what if she was alone with a stranger in this luxurious bedroom. She glanced at the painting again.

It was all worth it, wasn't it?

She took another sip and felt her confidence grow. *Who cares if he brought me up here to seduce me? This is the sort of thing that happens to Shelly, not me. If this is what it feels like to be coveted, I'll take it.*

He took the glass from her and placed it on the lacquered wooden cabinet facing the bed. Then he held out his hand.

"Would you honor me with this dance?" he all but whispered.

Cat bit her lip. This entire scenario was absurd: being in here, with this man, in this room... And now, he wanted to dance with her.

And yet...

She placed her hand in his, and he started to lead immediately.

Cat wasn't much of a dancer, and she certainly wasn't familiar with ballroom steps. Still, she found herself moving effortlessly. Her feet seemed to know what to do as the two of them started to circle around the room.

She wrapped her arm around his neck, just as his hand rested in the small of her back. They started off touching only lightly, but after a few steps, she found herself firmly in his grasp.

It didn't occur to her anymore to question what was going on.

This was amazing. She felt like Cinderella dancing through her very own fairy tale. Did that mean that Alexander was her Prince Charming? *No, that would be ridiculous.* This was just a fling at a Halloween party. Nothing less, and nothing more.

She gazed up at him, at those deep black eyes, which somehow managed to convey more emotion than any other guy she'd ever been with. How she wished she could see the rest of his face. She let her gaze travel downward to the part of his face that wasn't obscured.

Full lips, slightly parted to reveal perfectly white teeth.

His pale skin was smooth, flawless, without the slightest hint of stubble, or even a razor burn. Did rich people have ways and means to skip the inconveniences normal guys often had to deal with? Perhaps he was wearing some kind of make-up.

He asked her questions, about her family, where she was from. She did her best to answer, as she observed his every move.

Even his scent was unique: sweeter, cleaner than other guys. Not that Cat thought regular guys were dirty; Alexander was just different somehow, in a way that she couldn't make sense of.

She wasn't sure how long they'd been dancing for when the music stopped, as did the two of them. But they didn't let go. If anything, Cat thought she could feel his arm tighten around her. Similarly, she clung on to his neck and stared into his eyes.

This was the moment of truth. Now, she would find out what else tonight would bring.

CHAPTER FOUR

When the music stopped, Alexander was painfully aware that the longer they stood there, holding each other, the more awkward things might get. And yet, he couldn't bring himself to let Catherine go.

Neither did she seem in any hurry to get out of his embrace. Instead, she looked up at him with those mesmerizing green eyes as though she was trying to tell him something.

In the centuries that he had been walking this earth, he had never really focused on human attraction as a subject of study. He'd preferred more philosophical topics.

Right now, he could have really used some extra knowledge to interpret Catherine's demeanor.

Of course, it wasn't difficult for a vampire to seduce a woman simply by keeping her under his spell. But something about her demanded for him to treat her honorably.

He wanted for this amazing woman to want him back.

So far, so good it seemed.

"The music has stopped," she remarked at last.

Alexander smiled subtly. "I can remedy that."

"No, I think that's enough dancing for one night," she responded.

And yet, she didn't make a move.

He allowed his gaze to rest on her curvaceous lips. She didn't wear much makeup, just a bit of lipstick and perhaps eyeshadow. Either way, she had a natural beauty to her that was more impressive than anything man-made could ever be.

As was her scent, actually.

Her hair was fragrant; it reminded him of that display of summer flowers in the painting they'd admired together only moments earlier. In her eyes he recognized the color of morning dew on a lawn in bright sunlight, something he hadn't seen for a very long time indeed.

At first it had been easy for him to be nocturnal, but as the centuries passed, he had come to miss little things like that. In Catherine, he saw all that and more. He saw life. He saw hope.

She tiptoed slightly, perhaps without even realizing that she had, bringing her face closer to his. Her eyelids fluttered and then shut.

This was his chance.

Alexander stopped thinking about what was happening and proceeded on instinct alone. He kissed her sweet lips, which parted almost instantly, allowing him a taste of her tongue.

Intoxicating.

Excitement overwhelmed him, or was it hunger? He wanted her so badly, it became hard to focus on anything else. His senses worked at a feverish pitch; the floral scent of her skin and hair continued to egg him on. The softness of her skin under his touch invited him in for more tactile explorations. But above all, the sound of her heartbeat as it sped up, the rush of blood running through her veins—it drove him to the edge of insanity.

How could he resist her?

He pulled back and looked down at the elegant curve of her neck. That was where her jugular was, throbbing as her body pumped around what promised to be the best meal of his life.

She opened her eyes, diverting his attention back to her face.

"I'm sorry, I didn't mean to," she stammered.

Alexander smiled. "Yes, you did. As did I."

She pressed her lips together but didn't avert her gaze.

He would resist the draw of her blood a little while longer. Something told him that once he started, he wouldn't be able to control himself, and the last thing he wanted was to harm her.

"Tell me more about yourself," he whispered, as he led her by the hand to the bed and gestured that she sit with him.

Catherine paused for a moment, then looked down at his hand, which still enclosed hers.

"Not much to tell..."

"What do you do?" Alexander suggested. That was all small talk, though. What he really wanted to know went much deeper than that. Her hopes and dreams, her outlook on the world. Those were the questions playing on his mind whenever he met someone new. Most of the time his talks with humans were research to him. This was something deeper.

"Well, you know where I'm from already. I just came up here to study. Now that that's over, I've been looking for work." She looked up at him, those pale green eyes practically begging for further affections.

Alexander reached out and ran his fingertip across her cheek. Such soft, perfect skin. Was she this pleasing to the touch all over?

"Let me guess, something to do with art?" Alexander said.

Catherine's gaze darted across the room at the painting. "Yes, that's right. I like to be around beautiful things. Art History was an obvious—"

Alexander couldn't resist any longer. He let go of her hand and cupped her face, pressing his lips against hers in an attempt to still his intense desire for her. It was no use, though. All their kisses did was fan the fire within him.

Apparently, she felt the same. Though she started off a bit shy and taken aback, soon her kisses competed with his in intensity and passion. They wrapped their arms around each other and fell back onto the bed to take things to the next level.

———•◆•———

Cat still couldn't believe where she was, and who she was with. This simply wasn't the sort of thing that happened to girls like her.

Shelly, sure. She could imagine Shelly in a room like this. With a guy like Alexander.

His hands were all over her now. And it felt so good.

While she'd started off nervous, the passion he showed had quickly encouraged her to let go too. It was all so unlike her, so deliciously naughty. She needed a night like this, perhaps more than she'd ever allow herself to admit.

It had been a while since she'd been on a date. Alexander reminded her how nice it was to feel wanted.

He caressed her curves, while she explored his toned, muscular body through his clothes. Everything felt like it had fallen into place. There was just one catch: she wasn't quite certain what her mysterious lover looked like.

And she couldn't contain her curiosity any longer.

Cat reached out for his mask and carefully lifted it off. For a moment, she was mesmerized by his symmetrical features, his high cheek bones and almost ivory skin. He was beautiful. Just like...

Oh my God.

Cat pulled back in a panic. He looked identical to the man in the painting she'd found herself staring at earlier. The hunting scene hanging by the staircase.

The work of art that was so eerily realistic, she'd found it impossible to ignore.

And as she'd passed it by on the way up here, she'd seen it up close. From the patina and subtle cracks in the paint to the style of frame, she'd been certain it had to be hundreds of years old.

How could a painting that old depict a man who was right here and now? It was impossible.

She forgot to breathe and tried to scramble away from him.

He was trouble.

He was dangerous.

She could feel it so keenly now. The nerves she'd felt before were trying to tell her that something was wrong. And she'd brushed those feelings away because she loved the attention.

All of this, it *had* been too good to be true. This man wasn't of this world. This wasn't possible.

Cat's heart raced now. Her chest felt tight, like she was about to asphyxiate.

All the while, Alexander seemed oblivious to the change in her. While she tried to get away from him, he followed and tried to kiss her again.

She pressed her lips together tightly and evaded his grasp, stumbling off the bed, landing right in between her shoes. Her bag was waiting on the dresser. She grabbed all her things and didn't look back once as she fled the room.

"What happened?" she heard Alexander's voice behind her. "Catherine?"

She didn't owe him an explanation. Her heart beat so fast she could feel it in her throat and temple. All she needed to do right now was get away.

And so she sprinted down the stairs, her shoes still in

her hand. A few heads turned in her direction as she made it back to the entrance hall, but she didn't care. Where was Shelly?

Cat scanned her surroundings and spied her talking to some guy in a pirate costume just inside the reception room. *Thank God.*

"Shelly," Cat said. "Shelly!"

Shelly frowned as she turned to face her and noticed the state she was in: messed up hair, bare feet. "What's going on?"

"We've got to go," Cat said.

Shelly glanced at the man she had been in conversation with before, then back at Cat. "Why? What happened?"

"I don't have time to explain right now. Please. Just trust me. Let's go."

Shelly turned to her companion. "Excuse us for a moment, all right?" Then she took Cat's arm and led her into a slightly quieter corner of the room.

"Did some guy attack you? Where is he? I'll sort him out!" Shelly demanded.

Cat just shook her head. "No, I agreed to go up there. That's not... Look, it's a long story. Can we please just go now?"

"So you weren't attacked?"

"No." *Not yet, anyway.*

"You're not hurt, are you? Are you okay?" Shelly asked.

Cat took a deep breath and looked down at her bare feet. *This must look pretty weird.*

In fact, people were already starting to stare at her. And now that she wasn't with Alexander anymore, the big realization she had about him seemed ludicrous. A man who was several hundred years old. That was stupid. Nobody would believe her, not even Shelly.

"I'm fine. I just want to go," Cat mumbled.

"I don't get you. You're fine—everything's fine, but you want to leave. The costume competition hasn't even started yet and I think I have a decent chance here." Shelly squinted and cocked her head to the side. "You never really wanted to come to this party anyway. Is that it?"

Meanwhile, the man she'd been talking to earlier approached them and rested his hand on Shelly's shoulder. "I'm going to get something to drink. Can I get you ladies anything?" he asked.

Cat stared at him blankly. What was he thinking, interrupting them like that?

From Shelly's expression it was obvious that she didn't share Cat's outrage. Instead, she smiled and nodded. "Champagne would be lovely. Anything for you?" Shelly asked.

Cat shook her head. Whatever.

She had nothing. No explanation. No way to convince Shelly to go. If that was how it was going to go, fine!

"I'm going home. I'll see you whenever," Cat grumbled.

"Oh come on, don't be like that! Stay a little longer! It's only just getting started in here." Shelly pouted. "And the competition starts in a few minutes..."

"Whatever. I'm out." Cat put on her shoes and adjusted her hair before marching out of the room, as well as the house. Although she'd tried to make herself somewhat presentable, she could feel the stares of the other guests burning into her back.

If there ever was a walk of shame, this must have been what it felt like.

As the doors opened, a gust of cold air stung her skin, giving her goosebumps all over. Luckily, on the drive outside, several cabs waited. She got into the first one and breathed a sigh of relief as she shut the double door behind her.

"Shepherd's Bush, please."

CHAPTER FIVE

Why had she left like that? What had he done to spook her?

Alexander paced around the room, back and forth, for at least twenty minutes, as if somehow that would help provide an answer. Of course it didn't. It just made him more agitated.

Everything had gone so well. Until all of a sudden she turned completely pale, her eyes went wide with fear, and she'd fled. Had he accidentally shown his fangs?

He wasn't a regular womanizer like Michael was, but he wasn't that stupid either. No, it had to be something else...

Out in the hallway the large grandfather clock struck midnight, and Alexander couldn't contain his frustration any longer. This was his party and if the fun was over for him, it could bloody well be over for everyone. He burst through the door and down the stairs, when the first painting they'd discussed caught his eye.

Bloody hell!

Alexander stopped in his tracks halfway down and stared darkly at the portrait. He couldn't believe he hadn't put things together sooner. She'd left the moment she'd seen him without his mask on. She had *recognized* him. From this innocuous little hunting scene he'd kept around as a reminder of another life.

In all his years living here, he'd had plenty of humans over, mostly during events much like this one. Not one of them had ever put it together like she had.

Most humans were easy to fool and not all that perceptive. But Catherine wasn't like most humans.

"Okay, party's over!" Alexander raised his voice.

Some people at the bottom of the stairs turned to give him a disapproving look, then turned to each other again and continued their respective conversations.

"I mean it! Everybody out, now!" Alexander roared so loudly the chandelier above his head trembled, as did the windows beside the front door.

The music in the reception room stopped, as did all the chatter among the guests.

Within a split second, a disheveled looking Michael appeared at the top of the stairs. His hair was in a mess and he was shirtless; clearly Alexander's outburst had interrupted him with his two lady friends. If he was annoyed about the disturbance, he didn't show it.

"Go on, gather your belongings and make your way to the exit!" Michael shouted. Whatever his vices, the young vampire was loyal to a fault.

Alexander nodded his approval and turned to face the crowd again. The first people were on their way out, while whispering to one another.

This abrupt end to this year's famed Halloween event was going to be the fodder to many a gossip, no doubt. Alexander didn't care, though. He didn't care about any of these people who just came to drink the free champagne and eat the finger food.

The one person he cared about had already left, and he wasn't even sure why he cared. What was so special about Catherine?

As the humans left, all the vampires attending the party grouped around the bottom of the stairs waiting for some kind of explanation of what had happened. As they stared up at him, Alexander was reminded of their strange behavior when Catherine had just arrived. They'd all been able to smell her. Why?

What was it about this woman?

He ought to ask them, if only he thought he'd get an honest answer. Not from any of them, except perhaps Michael. But he had already found himself some company and retreated upstairs by the time Catherine had even arrived, so he probably hadn't noticed her presence at all.

The reception room and entrance hall quickly emptied out, leaving just the staff, who were frantically clearing up, and the vampires. Still, Alexander felt more agitated, not less.

"What are you all looking at? I asked everyone to leave. That includes you too!" he snapped.

Gillian, one of the more senior vampires in attendance, glared at him.

"Your behavior is completely unacceptable," she spat.

"This is my house and I get to behave how I like in it," he said.

They stared each other down, until Michael joined Alexander's side on the landing, causing Gillian to back off.

They couldn't afford a physical altercation, not with all the human staff still around. Tonight's events would make waves as it was. The last thing they needed was to be called in by the Council for outing themselves.

Gillian knew that better than anyone.

And so, even the immortals started to leave until only Michael remained.

"I might need a moment, if you know what I mean," he said, while looking in the general direction of the bedrooms upstairs.

Alexander nodded. That was the least he could do.

"Are you going to tell me what happened tonight?" Michael asked.

Alexander folded his arms. He wanted to. He ought to.

"All right. Join me in the library when you're ready."

Within the blink of an eye, Michael was gone, leaving Alexander alone with his thoughts again. He left behind the catering staff to do their jobs and retreated, a bottle of his finest aged brandy in hand. The library was always off limits to guests during events such as this one, allowing him one true refuge from all the activity that was still going on.

Alexander sat down in one of the leather arm chairs and poured himself a drink.

Of course, his metabolism didn't allow him to feel the

effects of alcohol, but he still enjoyed the ritual of it all. This was one of those little things that allowed him to feel at home, no matter how much the world around him had changed.

So he stayed in that chair, sipping the amber liquid from an antique crystal snifter he'd had in his possession for the better part of the century, until Michael turned up.

"Sorry about that. That took longer than I expected it to," Michael said as he took a seat in the arm chair next to Alexander.

"A drink?" Alexander asked.

Michael accepted his offer and took a sip.

"So what happened tonight?" he asked, after setting down his glass on the table between the two chairs.

"It's rather difficult to explain." Alexander folded his hands and stared straight ahead. He wasn't quite sure what had happened himself.

"This woman arrived; she was unlike any I've encountered before. Her presence seemed to affect every vampire in the room," Alexander started, and closed his eyes to relive the moments leading up to Catherine's sudden change of heart. "I approached her, made a little conversation, you know how it goes."

"Right."

"Then I took her upstairs, where we danced. Things were going so well. She'd made me feel things I haven't felt in a long time."

"And this was a human woman, who had affected you

so?" Michael's voice was laden with disbelief. Sure, he enjoyed the female form more than most, but he never got too involved with any of his marks.

Alexander sighed and opened his eyes again. It was all a game to Michael. He wouldn't understand.

"She wasn't vampire if that's what you're asking," Alexander said.

"Still, it all sounds bizarre."

"It was."

"And the others noticed her too? I'm almost sad I wasn't there to see her. Almost!" Michael winked at Alexander, who just shook his head.

They sat quietly for a while, giving Alexander more of a chance to relive his last moments with Catherine.

A loud bang on the door interrupted the silence. "Open up. Council business!" a firm female voice called out.

"Come in, Lucille!" Alexander sighed again. His outburst at the party had been unorthodox, but surely not serious enough to warrant an instant visit from the Council's enforcer?

The door swung open, revealing a petite, slender vampire, who marched in with her hand on her hip.

"What can I do for you, sister?" Alexander asked, while emptying his glass with one last sip.

"Alexander. Good to see you," Lucille said, then acknowledged Michael only with a curt nod.

"Well, unless you need me, I'll be upstairs," Michael said as he got up from his chair. The much younger vampire had never been comfortable in Lucille's presence. His quick escape would have been comical, had Alexander not had other things on his mind.

"Julius sends me," Lucille said as she took the seat Michael had just vacated.

Alexander poured himself another drink, then held up the bottle at Lucille, who shook her head. "I'll never know why you like this stuff."

Alexander shrugged and set the bottle down again.

"What does our dear maker want?" he asked.

"Word has spread fast about what happened at your little soirée this evening," Lucille started.

Alexander frowned. He had Gillian to thank for that, no doubt. The old hag loved to gossip, especially when she felt wronged somehow.

"What about it? I invited people over, and then I asked them to leave when the party was over."

Lucille shook her head and smiled subtly. "Brother, why so defensive? That's not what I'm here to discuss."

"Oh?" Alexander put his glass down and turned to face Lucille properly to observe her every move. They were brother and sister, in vampire terms. After Julius had made both of them, they had even spent their first century together.

But loyalties changed over the centuries. Who knew what Julius was up to nowadays? You couldn't fully trust another vampire, only yourself; time had taught Alexander as much.

Lucille smiled again. "We hear that one of your guests was very special indeed."

Catherine. They knew about Catherine.

Alexander tried his best to feign surprise. "Is that so? Special how?"

"Don't tell me you didn't notice. We hear you were the only one to interact with her!" Lucille argued.

Alexander remained quiet. So Gillian *had* told them everything. This was the last time she'd be invited to one of his parties.

"No matter. What we really want to know is: where is she now?" Lucille asked.

"How would I know? She left."

"Right. Well she came by an invitation somehow. Where does she live?" Lucille pressed him again.

"I never saw her before tonight. Someone must have passed their invitation on to her," Alexander said, while looking Lucille straight in the eye. One of the reasons Julius had appointed her as enforcer was that she had an uncanny talent for uncovering the truth. She could always tell when someone was lying. Luckily for Alexander, he truly had no idea where Catherine might have gone.

"Well, I'm sorry I couldn't be of more help to you or Julius... But are you going to tell me what it is that makes her so special?" Alexander asked.

Lucille pursed her lips like she usually did when she was mulling something over.

"Well, I suppose there's no harm in telling you, brother.

You have been trying to cooperate after all."

Alexander leaned forward in anticipation. Any information that allowed him to understand Catherine better might help him track her down. If Julius and the Council were after her, that was bad news. She needed to be warned.

"Every so often a human female is born with blood so potent it has a profound effect on all vampires. It might be a mutation of some sort; we're not sure without further study. These women are called Blood Brides. So as you might imagine, having her walk around the city is bad news. Any vampire who tries to feed on her will not be able to control themselves. We could be outed, or worse."

Alexander's jaw tensed up. Lucille's explanation made sense. That was why Catherine had attracted everyone's attention the moment she walked in.

"So what do you plan to do once you find her?" Alexander asked, though he wasn't sure he wanted to know the answer.

"That's not for me to say. Julius ordered me to find her, so that's what I'm doing. Vampire lore has it that Vlad the Impaler was seduced by a Blood Bride sent in by his enemies. That's what led to his ultimate defeat. Hence reports of a real life Blood Bride have got everyone in the Council very worried indeed. If she fell into the wrong hands..." As Lucille spoke, Alexander couldn't detect any sign that she was lying or holding anything back.

"Fair enough. Thank you for sharing this with me. I'll

keep my eyes open for her. And if you need anything, don't hesitate to ask," Alexander said.

Lucille smiled and got up. "Thank you, brother." She nodded at him, then made a quick exit, leaving Alexander alone with his thoughts again.

If the Council considered Catherine a threat, Alexander had to make sure he found her first.

CHAPTER SIX

Cat hadn't waited up for Shelly after reaching home, not on purpose anyway. Instead, she'd gone straight to bed and tried to get some rest. But sleep didn't find her; she kept tossing and turning until she ended up on her back, staring at the ceiling.

How dare Shelly ignore her concerns and stay behind? If she was going to act like that, she could have gone on her own in the first place. But no, Cat had to come along, and she'd wasted a handsome amount on a stupid costume too.

Cat closed her eyes and there he was. Alexander.

She'd wanted to forget all about him, but for some reason her mind hadn't finished processing what had happened. She couldn't understand it at all.

Everything had been fine at first, even if completely bizarre. And then his mask came off.

In her memories, Cat thought she could see a scary red glow in his eyes. That was just fantasy, surely? Her brain had just embellished things to make him seem scarier, when actually he probably only shared a passing resemblance to the man in the painting, and his eyes had been the same damn color throughout.

She had completely overreacted and made a fool of herself.

No wonder Shelly hadn't entertained her craziness.

Cat wasn't sure how long she'd been lying in bed like this, berating herself for how she'd handled things. She could have been there still, in that luxurious bedroom, with a man who normally might not even have given her a second look. It had felt so good to feel his hands on her body, his lips on hers.

She'd panicked, plain and simple.

And now, she was almost convinced she'd made a huge mistake.

Elsewhere in their shared apartment, the click of the door lock signaled Shelly's return.

Cat took a deep breath and got out of bed. If she couldn't sleep anyway, she might as well talk things through with Shelly.

"Hey," Cat said, when she entered the living room.

Shelly blew into her hands and rubbed them together vigorously, then looked up.

"You won't believe what happened!" she blurted out.

Cat folded her arms. "Oh yeah?"

"I won!" Shelly grinned and handed over an envelope.

Cat opened it. Indeed, inside there was a check for the promised £1000.

"That's amazing, congratulations!" Cat gave Shelly a hug; the latter was so cold to the touch that it sent chills down Cat's entire body.

"You must be freezing. How about a cup of tea?" Cat suggested.

Shelly smiled and nodded. "That would be great."

Cat headed for the kitchen with Shelly hot on her heels. As the kettle boiled, she got the full rundown of how the costume competition went down, what everyone else was wearing, and who the three finalists were. The party ended right after, so Shelly had left with the man in the pirate costume.

The more Shelly talked, the easier it was for Cat to get swept up in her excitement. Why did she have to run before any of this happened? She should have been there, cheering Shelly on.

Of course, then Cat remembered what happened with Alexander and cringed. She'd handled that all wrong.

"So. Now that that's out of the way... Are you going to tell me what happened tonight?" Shelly asked, then brought her mug to her lips and took a first, tentative sip.

Cat took a deep breath and followed her example. The tea seemed to help give her the courage she needed to share her story.

"Moments after we arrived, this guy started talking to me," Cat began.

Shelly looked up, her eyes wide with curiosity. "What guy?"

"His name is Alexander. It was his party." Cat's voice tapered off into a whisper. It sounded so ludicrous out loud.

"You met the host? Holy shit, why didn't you say so earlier? You could have introduced me!" Shelly said.

Cat raised her hand in a calming gesture. "Are you going to let me tell the story or what?"

"Okay." Shelly put her index finger over her lips and nodded.

"All right then." Cat traced the rim of her mug with her finger while considering how best to continue. "Well one thing led to another..."

Shelly's eyes went even wider, but to her credit, she kept her comments to herself.

"I don't know what happened. Something felt wrong. I don't know if it was the champagne, or whatever. But for a moment, I was convinced that the guy wasn't who he said he was. I felt like I was in danger."

"Wow."

"Yeah. Well, that's when I ran downstairs and found you. And the rest you know."

"What was he like?" Shelly asked.

Cat rolled her eyes. Of course that was what Shelly had focused on.

"I dunno. Handsome, articulate, really posh. He was showing me some of the artwork around the house. And my God, he could dance. It was like we were floating."

Shelly tilted her head to one side, her eyes dreamy.

"I would have liked to meet that guy; Alexander, you say?"

Cat couldn't suppress a smile. "Alexander Broderick the Third."

Shelly let out a shrill giggle. "You're kidding me!"

Cat shook her head. "I swear, that's what he said his full name was."

"And you bailed just as you were starting to... you know?"

Cat cringed again, and stared into her tea rather than make eye contact. "Yes."

"That's... wow."

"Insane, right?" Cat whispered.

"Totally." Shelly took another sip. "I still don't get why you ran."

"Yeah. I don't quite understand it anymore either. It made sense at the time."

"Maybe the champagne didn't agree with you indeed. Or..." Shelly paused. "No, that doesn't make sense."

"What?"

"If he managed to spike your drink somehow, I doubt that's how you would have reacted. At least I've never heard of anything like it."

Cat shook her head. "He wouldn't do that."

"I thought you said he was dangerous?" Shelly asked.

Cat pressed her lips together. Yeah, she had said that. The whole situation was confusing and bizarre. Now that she was here, in the safety of their shared home, he didn't seem so dangerous anymore. The look in his eyes hadn't been threatening, it had been caring and protective.

"Well, anyway. I'm glad you're okay now," Shelly said.

Cat smiled briefly. "Yeah. I'm glad too."

Now that she'd shared her side of things, finally it

seemed that all the excitement was catching up with her. Cat couldn't suppress a yawn and put her now empty mug down on the kitchen counter. "I'm going to bed. See you tomorrow."

Shelly patted her on the shoulder. "Goodnight, sleepyhead."

Cat nodded and made her way back to her bedroom. Funny, how she'd gone from wide awake to overcome with drowsiness in seconds. Perhaps someone had put something into her drink tonight.

She didn't think about it anymore. As soon as she was safely tucked in, it was like a black cloud descended over her and knocked her out.

———◆———

The crowd split and formed a circle around them. Cat looked at Alexander, whose previously black eyes had started to glow red. This time, she wasn't scared though. It just seemed... normal.

"May I have the honor of this dance?" Alexander glanced down at Cat's hand.

She placed it in his as if it was the most natural thing in the world.

The music came out of nowhere, and they started to dance. They twirled and swayed effortlessly. Although Cat was wearing heels, she felt completely steady, until gradually her legs and then her whole body started to feel weightless.

Alexander kept his gaze locked on Cat's face, drawing her closer into his arms as they floated up off the dance floor, several feet above the rest of the guests.

Cat couldn't hear anything except the seductive tones of the violins that grew ever louder.

That was when she caught a glimpse of that painting, over Alexander's shoulder, and recognized him in it.

"That's you, isn't it?" Cat asked, only this time, she didn't feel any fear.

Alexander smiled briefly. "You're very perceptive. You know your art."

Cat couldn't keep her eyes off the painting, until they twirled again and she could no longer see it. Then she looked at Alexander's face again. Handsome, flawless. His smooth skin gave the impression that he was made entirely of the finest Italian marble.

She'd never seen a man quite like him.

Was he even a man? They were floating high above the shiny parquet floor of the entrance hall now. And she was pretty sure she wasn't the reason they'd started to defy gravity.

She closed her eyes.

"You smell delicious," Alexander whispered in her ear. The tickle of his breath against the side of her neck gave her goosebumps.

She didn't respond, just held on to him tighter.

Butterflies collected in her stomach, fluttering more violently with every passing second until she could hardly contain her excitement anymore.

"You're mine," he whispered.

She smiled. She wanted to be his.

Cat opened her eyes and found that their surroundings had changed. No longer were they in the same room; instead he had somehow carried her upstairs into that same bedroom without her knowing.

She gently landed on her back on the bed with Alexander on top of her. He kissed and nibbled at the side of her neck, until suddenly a sharp pain caused her heart to skip a few beats.

He pulled back and looked down at her.

She could see the blood dribbling down from the corner of his mouth. Like red wine against white marble.

He dove down and attacked her neck again.

It hurt, but it didn't alarm her as much as it excited her further.

It was a beautiful, sweet sort of pain.

She writhed against the sheets in ecstasy, desperate for Alexander to continue whatever it was he was doing. He sucked at her skin, which satisfied her much like scratching an itch, or like a long-awaited sneeze. The comparisons that entered her mind didn't do the feeling justice.

She knew it was wrong.

She knew it was dangerous.

And yet, she didn't want it to stop.

A shrill sound filled the air. She covered her ears and shut her eyes, but the repetitive, high pitched beeping continued to increase in volume until it overwhelmed her completely.

Finally, Cat opened her eyes, only to find the familiar sights of her very own bedroom. It had all been a dream. She turned off the alarm and fell back into the pillows. Ten o'clock already. If it wasn't for the alarm, she might have slept even longer.

The side of her neck still tingled, which was odd. Cat instinctively reached for it and rubbed it a few times to make the feeling go away.

And that wasn't the only body part which still felt the after-effects of her strange dream, the details of which had already begun to fade. Her whole body seemed on edge; she was tense, aroused.

What a mess. She'd ruined the only shot she'd ever have with Alexander, and now she was obsessing about him in her sleep?

Cat took a deep breath and got up. She didn't have time for this. Tomorrow would be the first day at her new job, and she had to keep her wits about her if she wanted to make a good impression. But first, she had to head to the shops to collect a few last minute items.

This was her first real job, not counting the part time work she'd done in the past. Her wardrobe really needed the help.

CHAPTER SEVEN

Alexander hadn't gotten much rest all day. He kept thinking about what Lucille had told him.

Catherine was a Blood Bride, and now everyone was after her. And when he wasn't consciously thinking about that, he'd been replaying every moment he'd spent with Catherine in his head, as well as some scenarios that hadn't yet come to pass.

Part of him wished she'd never turned up at his party. Another, much more insistent part of him was glad that she had.

She'd made him feel alive during the short time they'd spent together.

No way was he going to let anyone, including the Council, harm the one woman who had made him feel that way, centuries after he'd been turned.

He had to intervene somehow.

He got up early—in vampire terms—just before sundown. The black-out blinds on all the windows kept him safe enough to move around freely inside the house.

So he headed straight for the library.

Somewhere in this vast collection of old books, there had to be some information, some mention of what Lucille had told him.

How would he help Catherine if he didn't know for

sure what he was dealing with?

He owned an extensive selection of historical manuscripts, dating back over half a millennium. Most of the books he'd acquired and displayed had been chosen more for their decorative value than anything else. He'd never actually read them. That was about to change.

Alexander's best bet would be texts about Vlad the Impaler. Most of the works in his collection were human accounts of history though, not vampire. No matter how many volumes he removed from their respective shelves and leafed through, Alexander couldn't find anything relevant.

It was no use.

After a couple of hours of failed research, he sat down in his leather arm chair and rested his head in his hands. This was hopeless.

"Still thinking about that woman?" a voice asked.

Alexander looked up and found Michael staring down at him.

"Have you ever heard of a Blood Bride?" Alexander asked.

Michael frowned. "No."

"Wonderful." Alexander sat back and stared at nothing in particular.

"So what's a Blood Bride, then?" Michael sat down next to Alexander as he asked the question.

"In a nutshell: a human woman with very special blood."

Michael nodded in silence and folded his hands.

"Have you googled it?" he finally asked.

Alexander gave him a skeptical look. "What do you mean *have I googled it?*"

"Well, that *is* the fastest way of looking things up nowadays." Michael gestured at the piles of old volumes stacked up everywhere. "Especially since your books clearly haven't been of much help."

Alexander still stared at the younger vampire, who finally retrieved a smartphone from his pocket and started tapping away at the screen.

"Here. Try it." Michael handed him the device.

He had already opened a search, though the results didn't look promising. It was all horror movies and cheap fiction. Alexander raised an eyebrow and held back a snide remark as he scrolled through the first page, then switched to the image view.

It would be easy to give up already, but he was determined to check out everything, if only to be able to genuinely tell Michael how stupid his suggestion had been.

Page after page of blood-splattered women in wedding dresses awaited him. He scrolled and scrolled, through what must have been thousands of images, when the very last result caught his eye: an old illustration, on what looked like parchment.

It was a woman wearing what looked to be a traditional sort of frock and apron common among the lower classes during the end of the middle ages. Surrounding her stood a

few humanoid creatures with monstrous faces and fangs—
not a very accurate depiction of vampires, but clear
enough to be recognizable.

Underneath, in Gothic style lettering, it read: Bride of
Blood.

Alexander clicked through and started to read. The
entire website contained extracts from an old book the
author merely referred to as the *Encyclopedia of Myth and
Magick*. It wasn't complete, but the section on Blood
Brides was more informative than anything else Alexander
had found.

"I don't believe it," he mumbled.

"Found something?" Michael's voice was loaded with
glee.

Alexander glanced up and found that Michael was
grinning at him. "Fine. You were right. Listen to this—"

Alexander held the phone up and started to read aloud.

"The existence of Blood Brides was first documented
by the Ancient Egyptians, who believed that they were
sent down by the gods to cleanse the world of evil. The
presence of one of these women would inevitably attract
all creatures of the night, making them easy to control
and/or capture. What is notable about these women is that
they themselves are unaware of their powers and often do
not understand the attention they attract, yet at the same
time, they can be extremely perceptive when it comes to
the world at large."

Alexander looked up. That was it. Catherine had

noticed that it was him in the hunting scene painting after all.

"In ancient Egypt, as soon as a girl was identified as a Blood Bride, she was sent off to be raised by priestesses of Isis at one of the many temples dedicated to her worship. The practice of sending Blood Brides away to become priestesses to a female deity may have extended into Roman times. Some historians believe that the Vestal Virgins of Rome in fact always had at least one Blood Bride among their ranks. There is no conclusive evidence to support this theory, though. More recently, mythical scholars have formulated a theory that the occurrences of Blood Brides in the general populace is directly linked to the amount of supernatural activity at any given time, or in any given region. It therefore follows that a Blood Bride would only be born during times of hardship or when humanity is under threat from evil forces. Therefore, it is thought that during the Great Plague, Blood Brides were a lot more common than they are today. Over the centuries, all manner of tests have been devised to identify if a woman is a Blood Bride, most notably—"

Inconveniently, that was all there was. The method for identification and specifics regarding Vampirism and Blood Brides were missing.

Alexander gave the phone back to Michael.

"So you think that's what she was?" Michael asked.

Alexander shrugged. "That's what Lucille said she was. That's why they're after her; they think she's a threat to the

Council."

"Do you think she's a threat?"

Alexander folded his hands. "I just know that the moment she walked in, every vampire in the room turned to look at her."

Michael looked down at his phone, and scrolled back and forth a few times. "None of this explains how to defeat her powers, though."

Alexander turned to give Michael a disapproving look. "I don't want to defeat her! I want to keep her safe!"

"Oh." Michael turned off the phone and put it down on the table between them. "Well then, perhaps your books will be some use after all. Isn't there some law that prevents any vampire from harming another vampire's consort?"

Alexander waved Michael's suggestion away. He'd thought of that in passing already. "That only works if the intended is willing and not under hypnosis. You forget that this woman *fled* last night."

That wasn't the only problem, though. "I don't even know her full name. How will I track her down?" Alexander mumbled to himself.

Michael knew better than to answer that last, hypothetical question, so they both sat in silence for a while with Alexander lost in thought.

His thoughts moved back to last night, and the woman Catherine had arrived with. She seemed more extroverted, more of a social butterfly. Perhaps some of his other guests knew her.

He didn't even notice Michael had left his side, until the latter came back carrying a large envelope.

"Mail for you."

Alexander was about to discard it when he noticed the logo in the corner.

Sotheby's latest auction catalog.

As cliché as it was, perhaps some high end shopping might take his mind off things.

Michael grabbed his phone off the table and started tapping away at it; his expression suggested that the time for research had passed. The only thing he would be looking for now was a companion to spend the night with.

"Well, I'm off. I'll see you later," Michael mumbled a few moments later.

Alexander waved at him absentmindedly while leafing through the catalog. Nothing inspired him until he reached the very last page of the publication.

Anyone else might not realize what they were looking at, but Alexander did. Three pieces of old parchment, torn from one side as if they had been ripped out of a book and mounted in glass frames. If it wasn't for the illustration on the first page, he might not even have given it a second look.

He did a double-take on the description, then got up and headed straight for the land-line phone to RSVP for the upcoming auction.

Then he settled back down with the catalog and studied

the image that had caught his attention in more detail using a magnifying glass to boost his already powerful vision. The illustrations bore an uncanny resemblance to the image he'd just found on Michael's phone. The lettering also followed the same style. Sadly, the image wasn't detailed enough for Alexander to decipher the writing within.

He had no choice but to attend that auction, win the bid, and study these pages in person after.

Alexander sat back and closed his eyes.

Cat smiled at him, innocently, as though she had no idea of the effect she had on him. His whole being ached for her; he wanted to hold her, love her, keep her away from all the evil in the world. She twirled a lock of her long, dark brown hair around her index finger and turned away. Alexander reached out for her arm, but she slipped away. A terrifying, guttural cry pierced the silence; it took him a moment to realize that he was the one who had screamed.

Alexander tightened his grip on the armrests of his chair, stopping only when the leather under his right thumb gave way and tore.

Great. This was the second time in 24 hours that he'd accidentally destroyed his property while under the influence of Catherine, the supposed Blood Bride.

Alexander ran his fingertip across the torn leather and got up. The longer he sat here on his own, the closer he would come to losing his mind.

All this research, all these books, and none of it would help with his main problem: he still didn't know who or where she was. He had no choice but to go out there and do the necessary footwork to track her down.

Alexander left the house in a hurry, only to wander the city aimlessly all night. He crossed Kensington, Paddington, Mayfair, and Soho, but there was no sign of her or her unique scent anywhere.

If only he got somewhere near enough, his nose would pick up on her and lead him to her exact location. He knew that.

He just didn't know exactly where to look.

Just before dawn, he had no choice but to suspend the search.

CHAPTER EIGHT

Today was the big day.

Cat had woken up a bundle of nerves, after a restless night that featured even more unwanted dreams and fantasies. The star actor in all of them: Alexander. It was as though the thought of him simply refused to leave her be. Even when she was awake, he was right there, in her mind's eye, every time she blinked.

How am I going to concentrate? Cat rubbed her eyes and got out of bed. She stumbled into the bathroom to have a shower.

When she got out, she felt slightly better, but still listless. Back in her bedroom, she put on the outfit she'd laid out the night before, and did her hair, then she made her way toward the kitchen for a much needed caffeine boost.

Shelly was still in bed, it seemed—her shift wouldn't start until ten o'clock—so their apartment was eerily quiet. Cat tiptoed around the kitchen to prepare her packed lunch, when inevitably, she spilled a big dollop of mayonnaise on the front of her blouse.

"Dammit!" Cat cursed under her breath as she tried to wipe it clean.

It was no use, the stain was still visible.

She dumped the sorry excuse of a sandwich she'd made

into a Tupperware box, and rushed back into her room to change.

A knock on her door interrupted her.

"Hey..." Shelly stuck her head inside. "Shouldn't you be on your way by now?"

Cat checked the time on her phone. Shelly was right. "Crap. I spilled something. I can hardly turn up on my first day with a mayo stain on my left boob."

"Calm down. Take a breath," Shelly said as she stepped inside. "Let's see... Wear this one."

She held up a simple white blouse.

Cat sat down on the bed. "That's all wrinkled!"

"So what?" Shelly held it up into the light. "You're wearing a jacket on top. Nobody will be able to tell."

Cat sighed and held out her hand. "Fine."

She quickly changed into the new shirt and buttoned up her blazer to hide the offending wrinkles.

"Now go. You look fine," Shelly said. "And you'll do fine too. You have nothing to worry about!"

Cat smiled bleakly. "I hope so."

"I know so. Now go before you're late on your first day!"

That was all Cat needed to hear to gather all her stuff in a hurry and head for the door.

What a start to such an important day, she thought as she rushed toward the main road. As soon as she'd run down the steps to the tube platform, she saw the tail end of the train just as it was pulling away.

Bloody great.

———◆———

At least she wasn't late.

Despite everything, Cat had arrived at her new place of employment with about a minute to spare. She'd wanted to be early, of course, but you couldn't have everything in life, as her mom liked to say.

Sotheby's, one of the world's most prestigious auction houses, and *the* place to be for an art history graduate such as herself. She knew she wouldn't be in charge of anything important, but it was a privilege to be in this building, surrounded by so much wealth and beauty.

"Catherine?" A stern looking woman in her forties carrying a clipboard approached.

Cat recognized her from the first round of interviews. She took a step forward and offered her hand for a greeting. "Yes, Mrs. Pryce."

"Miss!" the woman corrected her, glancing down at Cat's hand, then turning away without shaking it. "Follow me."

Cat swallowed hard. That wasn't a great start. She held on tightly to her handbag and followed Ms. Pryce, who marched past the reception, through the corridors, and down the stairs leading into the basement at a dazzling pace, which Cat had trouble matching in her shoes.

"I assume I don't need to explain to you what it is we do here?" Ms. Pryce asked as she paused in front of a nondescript door.

"No, that won't be necessary," Cat mumbled. How was she meant to address this woman, Ma'am? No, that seemed risky, considering her earlier misstep.

"You'll be working in here, under Desmond's guidance, cataloging lots and their performance at auction."

Cat nodded. "No problem. I'm good at—"

Ms. Pryce shot her a blank look.

"Cataloging," Cat completed her sentence in a low mumble.

Of all the bosses in the world, she seemed to have hit the jackpot.

Cat glanced over at the woman, who impatiently tapped her foot and folded her arms while looking her up and down. Damn. Had she noticed her blouse was wrinkled? Or did she generally disapprove of her outfit?

Cat reached out for the knob, when the door opened on its own, revealing a frazzled looking man about Cat's age.

"Whoa, I'm sorry," he said, as he took a step back.

"Hi. I'm Cat. It's my first day." Cat stretched out her arm at him.

"Desmond." The man reluctantly shook her hand, then glanced over to Cat's left. "Good morning, Ms. Pryce."

"I'll leave you to it," Ms. Pryce said, and turned on her heel. The click-clack of her heels against the concrete floor echoed against the walls as she left, making a deafening racket.

"Well... Nice to meet you, Desmond," Cat said.

Desmond avoided eye contact and adjusted his thick-rimmed glasses. Clearly he wasn't a people person. "Uhh, yeah. Come in."

"Is she always like this?" Cat whispered, mostly to herself.

Desmond smiled bleakly. "You have no idea."

Cat reciprocated and breathed a sigh of relief. At least she wasn't all alone in this place. And with a bit of luck, they'd be working on whatever it was they were supposed to be working on without too much interference from Ms. Pryce, who probably had more important things to do.

This is only the beginning, Cat told herself. *Everyone starts at the lowest rung.*

"Let me show you what we do here," Desmond said as he waved her over.

Cat scanned the room. It was plain, like any other basement in any other building. Nothing here suggested that they were underneath one of the most prestigious auction houses in the world.

"You been here long?" It was all Cat could think of to make conversation.

"Three years," Desmond said.

His answer made her heart sank. Working your way up through the ranks clearly took a long time here. Still, this was the only job she'd been offered after applying pretty much everywhere. She was determined to make it work.

"So these racks here contain binders of old catalogs,

from before we started digitizing them. The newer ones can be seen from this computer." Desmond pointed at a workstation that looked to be at least ten years old.

"We need to prepare materials for upcoming auctions. The format is always the same: a high-res image and a detailed description. Check the previous catalogs for ideas on what to include. Once you're done with each lot, move it out of the inbox and into 'processing.'"

"Understood."

Cat took a seat in front of the desk with the computer and started poking around in the upcoming lots while Desmond explained the editing and publishing process. She was only half listening to him as pictures of exquisite artwork and antiques popped up on her screen, distracting her.

Would she get to actually see any of these items? She hoped that she would.

Within minutes, the reservations she'd had about Ms. Pryce and her prospects in this job faded, and she became absorbed in her work.

———— ◆ ————

"Hey," Cat greeted Shelly as she came into the living room.

"Hey! How did it go? Did you manage to get there on time? Tell me everything!" Shelly demanded as she plopped down on the sofa without even taking her coat off.

Cat sat back and pinched the bridge of her nose. It had

been a long day. Annoyingly, as soon as she closed her eyes, random glimpses of Alexander appeared before her again. Today had gone so well! She hadn't thought of him at all until she got home.

"Yes, I was on time, but oh my God, my boss is horrible!" She turned to face Shelly, who looked concerned. "Well, one of them is. The guy I'm working with directly, Desmond, he's okay. But the woman who was there at the interview... Wow."

"Okay... Well, no one ever said it was going to be easy." Shelly rubbed the side of her neck, just underneath the collar of her coat.

"True, that."

"And what's the job all about?" Shelly asked.

Cat pulled her legs up and wrapped her arms around them. That was how she stayed as she told Shelly about her work in so much detail that her eyes glazed over.

"Well, that sounds interesting." Shelly sounded unconvinced after Cat had finished her account.

"It is, actually. Not something I want to do forever, but for now it's all right."

Again, Shelly reached for her neck, scratching at it more vigorously this time.

"Are you all right?" Cat asked.

"Huh?"

"Your neck."

Shelly stopped scratching and fidgeted with her collar. "It's nothing. Just a little itchy."

Cat leaned across and pushed Shelly's collar down to take a closer look.

Her neck was red with scratch marks, but underneath, she could just about make out two brighter dots against Shelly's otherwise fair skin.

"It's a bit late in the season for mosquito bites," Cat mumbled.

Shelly shrugged. "With global warming and all, who knows? Anyway, what are you sitting around here for? You've got a job, and survived the first day. This calls for some celebration!"

Cat blinked a few times. "What do you mean?"

"Oh come on! You didn't think I'd just let this pass, did you? Get up, we're going out!"

Cat inhaled sharply, then held her breath. It had been a tiring day. She rubbed her eyes and was instantly confronted with those same visions of Alexander she'd been battling since the party. Every time she saw him in her mind, the visions were accompanied by larger and larger doses of melancholy. She had really messed up that night.

Ugh. Perhaps the distraction would do her good. She stretched her legs, then slipped her feet into the shoes she'd discarded underneath the coffee table.

"Fine. Where are we going?" Cat got up and looked to Shelly for instructions.

The latter shrugged. "Pub on the corner? We won't make it too late. Wouldn't want you to turn up on your second day nursing a hangover."

"Fair enough." Cat put on her coat and off they went.

The walk from their apartment complex to the pub was short and through a relatively well-lit and safe part of the neighborhood. Still, Cat turned around at least three times to look behind them.

"What's up with you?" Shelly asked finally.

Cat stopped and scanned the street behind them much more carefully now. Nobody. There was absolutely nobody around.

"I thought I heard something," Cat lied. She hadn't heard a damn thing. And neither had she seen anything. Still, she couldn't fight the feeling that there was someone out there, watching her.

She must be more stressed out than she thought.

"Maybe it was a cat or something," Cat mumbled and pressed on toward their destination: the brightly lit building at the end of the road. It took hardly a minute longer for them to arrive and Shelly to push the door open.

As soon as Cat entered, she started to relax. It was warm in here, cozy. Being a weekday, and that too Monday, the pub was quiet, with just a handful of regulars playing darts in the far corner. She breathed a sigh of relief and started unbuttoning her coat to get more comfortable.

They headed straight for the bar and ordered two pints as well as some dinner to share.

"Hey, why don't you tell me more about this Desmond

guy?" Shelly suggested as she plopped down in one of the tatty looking armchairs surrounding one of the empty tables.

Cat let out a chuckle. "Really. *That's* what you want to know?"

"Look, I don't know anything about art, but I do know about men. So yeah, that's what I want to know. Cheers." Shelly grinned and raised her glass.

"Fine. Whatever makes you happy. Cheers." Cat raised her glass too, then took a sip and told Shelly everything.

No matter how hard she tried, though, Cat couldn't fully banish Alexander from her thoughts, nor the regret she felt. If only she could turn back time.

CHAPTER NINE

Alexander paced back and forth in the grand hall outside the meeting room of the Vampire Council. His footsteps echoed against the marble clad walls, which didn't help settle his concerns. What a waste of time. He didn't even know anything.

Ever since Lucille had shown up the night of the party, he knew that it was likely Julius would call him in. Alexander was the one who had interacted the most with Cat, after all. And Julius enjoyed the ritual of it all: calling in his subjects for so-called audiences, to coerce them into doing his bidding.

That was what this was, no doubt: a reminder that Alexander had no choice but to cooperate. The Council didn't tolerate insubordination.

The heavy wooden doors swung open and Lucille appeared. "You can come in now," she said.

Alexander nodded and kept his shoulders and back as straight as possible as he marched in. Lucille was a walking lie detector, sure, but convincing Julius could be even more difficult. The years had made him cynical and suspicious; unfortunately right now, he had good cause to be.

"Alexander, how lovely of you to show your face around here!" Julius called out and waved him closer from the large throne-like chair at the opposite end of the hall.

Alexander glanced around and suppressed an eye roll. The Council—especially under Julius—really did like to make a statement. Of course they'd picked an old cathedral to host their meetings and deliberations. Everything, from the tall stained glass windows and the crude forged iron chandelier, right down to the Gothic wooden throne Julius sat on, had a clear purpose: to impress and intimidate.

"Of course. I came as soon as I heard you wanted to see me," Alexander said.

Julius folded his hands in his lap and looked him up and down.

"You look well. The 21st century has been good to you."

"Thank you. You look well yourself."

Julius waved away Alexander's forced compliment.

"Enough with the niceties. You know what I want to talk about, don't you?"

"The Blood Bride," Alexander said.

Julius' eyes lit up when he heard those all-important words. If he and the Council were indeed threatened by this woman's special powers, he had a strange way of showing it.

"That's right. Of all the times and places to come across a rare and magnificent creature like her, imagine my surprise to hear one just happened to attend one of your little parties," Julius mused. He leaned forward and gestured at the two guards by the door, as well as Lucille, who stood just to the right of Alexander.

"Leave us. I wish to speak to Alexander in private."

Alexander didn't need to turn around to know everyone had instantly sprang into action. The sound of departing footsteps spoke volumes. As soon as the heavy doors creaked back into position, Julius gestured at him again.

"Come closer, my son."

Alexander walked up toward what would have been the altar of the old church, where Julius' throne now sat. He kept his head bowed slightly, following the proper etiquette when approaching the Principis, or leader, of the Council.

"No need for formalities, my son. Look at me," Julius spoke firmly.

Alexander did as asked, and made eye contact with the much older vampire. There was a change in him from the last time they'd spoken. Normally, Julius appeared calm above everything, reserved. Unless provoked, he kept his emotions to himself. Not so now. His eyes were eager and bright.

"Please tell me exactly what happened that night. When did you first realize what she was?"

Alexander took a moment to collect his thoughts. He'd rehearsed what to say in his head, but now that he was faced with his maker, he suddenly found it a little difficult to walk the line between being compelled to follow his orders, and the intense urge he felt to protect Catherine.

"I didn't know until Lucille told me. All I knew was that she was different from the others."

Julius nodded in agreement. "Ah, yes. I imagine she would have been different. Everyone could tell as much once she walked in."

Alexander nodded. "Yes. I noticed everyone looking in her direction."

"So what was she like?" Again, Julius looked more excited than threatened, rousing Alexander's suspicion even further.

"She seemed completely unaware of how special she was," Alexander said. He tried his best not to let Julius' questions take him back to that night, as he knew it would make him vulnerable, but he couldn't help it. All the images he'd tried so hard to banish from his mind were flooding back.

"I spoke to her briefly, offered to show her around the house, since she'd shown an interest in some of the artwork," Alexander continued.

Julius nodded, encouraging him to go on.

"Upstairs, I asked her to dance, which we did." Alexander blinked a few times, completely aware that he was sharing more than he had intended to, but he couldn't help himself. He couldn't get the details of his much too brief encounter with Catherine out of his head.

If only he could've convinced her she was safe with him. If only she'd stayed.

"Did you taste her?" Julius asked.

The directness of the question dragged Alexander back to reality. He made eye contact once more and saw urgency, obsession.

"No, nothing like that," Alexander said, taken aback by what he had seen in his master.

"And you know nothing of her whereabouts, or any details that might be of help for us to track her down?"

Alexander shook his head, feigning disappointment. Sure, he was disappointed that he hadn't been able to track her down, but he was glad he wasn't in a position to hand her over to Julius.

"You're certain you didn't taste her, even by accident?" Julius pressed the issue again.

"No!" Alexander protested.

"Shame. I would have loved to know what that was like. I know you still have your youth to keep you entertained, but when you get to my age... Brand new experiences are hard to come by." Julius smiled absentmindedly.

Alexander balled his fists, then immediately released them again for fear of being found out. All this talk of drinking Catherine's blood made him uncomfortable. By all accounts, a vampire would lose control once they tasted her. Why fantasize about it? Why flirt with such immense temptation? Had Julius reached such heights of megalomania that he thought to be above Catherine's powers? Or did he simply not care about what would happen?

"So you think she's a threat to our kind?" Alexander asked, hoping to steer the conversation somewhere more agreeable.

Julius licked his lips before answering. "Well, the history books tell us that women such as her have immense power. It would be irresponsible not to investigate further."

Alexander found it hard to swallow his frustration. Julius was so clearly lying. He didn't want to contain some kind of threat; his questions as well as his whole demeanor had made it obvious that Julius wanted her for himself. What Alexander had seen in him wasn't curiosity or excitement; it was blood lust.

Principis of the Council or not, that was unacceptable. Catherine was his first, and even if she wouldn't have him, he would do everything in his power to keep her away from Julius. Her safety was at stake.

"Indeed, it would be irresponsible," Alexander remarked, glancing up at his maker's face again while keeping his posture as non-threatening as possible. He had to make sure his anger didn't show.

Fortunately, Julius barely seemed to be paying attention to Alexander. Instead, his focus was elsewhere. He already seemed enthralled by the prospect of capturing his very own Blood Bride, and the inevitable blood bath that would follow.

It was no wonder Julius had wanted all the other vampires to leave for this little chat. He must have known that he would share more than he intended to. Such was the effect Catherine had on almost everyone.

Nobody, not even the most powerful vampire on earth, was able to withstand her effect, whether she was physically present or not.

———◆———

Once Julius had dismissed him, Alexander didn't head home. He had already lost precious hours at the Council.

There was no time to waste; the city was vast, and finding one single human in all of that chaos was a huge task for a single vampire to take on. He didn't rest, he hadn't even fed all night, or the previous night.

The entire business with Catherine, and now the Council, was eating away at Alexander.

Where would a woman such as Catherine spend her evenings? Alexander checked out restaurants, bars, popular landmarks. It was no use. She was nowhere to be found.

Finally, when the first light of dawn threatened to cross the horizon, Alexander returned home, after another unsuccessful night.

"How did it go?" Michael looked up just as Alexander entered the library.

"No luck," Alexander said. He hated that he'd made no progress. With Julius obsessed, he wouldn't be the only one on the lookout. The Council had the manpower to cover much more ground in a much shorter time. And then there were the loyalists like Gillian. In this case, it was truly a case of one against many.

"I meant your meeting at the Council," Michael clarified.

"Oh." Alexander shook his head. "The plot thickens."

"How so?"

Alexander poured himself a drink and took a sip before answering.

"This whole Blood Bride business has everyone making fools of themselves." Alexander himself, of course, was included in this assessment. He would be the first one to go above and beyond to ensure Catherine's safety, when in fact she'd wanted nothing to do with him. It was pathetic, and completely unlike him.

He glanced over at Michael, who looked unconvinced. There was no point trying to explain any of it to him. Human women were only good for two things according to Michael: nourishment and entertainment.

Alexander looked down at the glass in his hand; its amber liquid seemed to glow in the subdued light of the library. He couldn't quite explain it to himself, either. Catherine had had a profound effect on even the most powerful vampire that currently walked this earth—and he hadn't even met her yet! How was it that while everyone seemed to just want to taste her, his own feelings were way more complicated than that?

It would have been easier had he just wanted her blood for himself, but it wasn't that. He wanted her whole being, but only if she wanted him too. But above all, he wanted her to be safe.

He took another sip and set his glass down on the table.

This urge was so alien to everything he'd known for centuries.

Was this what love was?

CHAPTER TEN

Cat had been working at Sotheby's for about a week when Desmond called in with the flu, leaving Cat to fend for herself.

For most of the day, Cat had done exactly the same as on previous days: hidden herself away down in the basement and completed some tasks Desmond had taught her.

The catalog prep was done for the week, and since they had an auction coming up, it was time to compile all upcoming lots in a spreadsheet so that after the event, they could enter how they'd performed. This data would be filed and compared to previous records of similar items.

It was all rather technical and boring on the face of it. Luckily, the lots themselves were so interesting that Cat managed to keep herself entertained.

She was almost done for the day when the door to the cramped little basement office swung open, revealing the last person she wanted to see.

"Catherine. Good, you're still here," Ms. Pryce said in a matter-of-fact tone.

"Yes, Ms. Pryce?" Cat responded almost on autopilot, as she saved her spreadsheet for the final time.

"I need you to stay behind." It wasn't a request; at least, it didn't sound like one.

Cat pressed her lips together and wondered what, if anything, she'd done wrong.

"The auction tonight. Normally Desmond would do this, but since he's not here..." Ms. Pryce clarified. "I need someone to observe the buyers, take notes on what they showed interest in, that sort of thing."

Cat's heart started to beat faster as soon as Ms. Pryce had said the word *auction*. This was her chance! And only a week into this job!

"Yes, of course I can attend tonight's auction!" Cat couldn't contain her excitement.

Ms. Pryce nodded. "I would expect no less. You might want to..." She gestured down at Cat's outfit. "Change into something more appropriate."

Cat looked down at her black trouser suit. *What's wrong with this?* It was very business-like, or so she thought.

"Yes, of course," Cat mumbled.

Ms. Pryce folded her arms and squinted at Cat. "A shift dress. Black. Heels." She nodded to make her point, then turned around and walked out again. "It begins at seven."

Cat exhaled sharply, having realized she'd been holding her breath for most of the time Ms. Pryce had been talking to her. A little black dress and heels. She could manage that. Hopefully.

A quick glance at the clock revealed she didn't have much time, certainly not enough for a round trip home. So Cat did the only thing she could think of; she called for help.

"Hey you!" Shelly answered the phone.

"You busy?" Cat asked, ignoring her greeting.

"Just tidying up and heading home, why?"

"I have a fashion emergency," Cat said. Those last two words would be irresistible to someone like Shelly, who lived to dress up.

"Tell me more!"

Cat smiled and explained the problem. She knew she could count on Shelly. The phone call was over in minutes with a promise that Shelly would be on the way as soon as possible with a suitable outfit from Cat's closet.

Cat sank back in her chair and breathed a sigh of relief. No way was she going to blow this opportunity.

In an effort to be well prepared for the auction—and to pass the time—Cat picked up a copy of tonight's catalog and started to read. She recognized the names of the lots from her earlier spreadsheet, but the images and descriptions were all new to her.

The selection of items was vast, from paintings to figurines and tea sets to large pieces of furniture. She had no way of knowing where exactly she would be during the auction itself, but Cat was determined to take a look at some of these items in person if she could manage it.

Half an hour must have passed, and Cat had read through most of the catalog, pausing on the final entry.

The picture showed some mounted pages which appeared to be from an old unnamed book as per the description. What a strange thing to be selling. Cat held up the catalog and looked at it more closely. She couldn't explain what it was, but something about this listing intrigued her more than any of the others.

For sure, this was one she would have to see up close.

Her phone rang, startling her. She put the catalog back down on the desk.

"Hey, Shelly!"

"I'm outside."

Cat hung up and made a beeline for the exit.

———◆———

Cat made it into the main hall upstairs ten minutes early. Ms. Pryce was already there, coordinating with other staff Cat had not met before.

"There you are." Ms. Pryce greeted Cat by handing her a clipboard and a pen.

"Yes, Ms. Pryce."

Ms. Pryce glanced down at Cat's outfit, like she had done earlier that evening already. There was nothing in her expression that signaled whether she approved or not.

Either way, it was too late to change anything. Cat smoothed her dress down with her free hand and awkwardly waited for her instructions.

"Within minutes, buyers will start to arrive. Jeremy and his people over here will ensure they find their seat and are given a paddle to make their bids with. Phone bids will be handled from over there beside the auctioneer's podium."

Cat nodded. It was a lot of information to take in and

Ms. Pryce's tone suggested that as usual, she expected Cat to learn quickly.

"What I want you to do is to observe any active bidders and take notes. You take down the number on their paddle, the lot number they bid on, and anything else that stands out to you. And I want you to take your own initiative on this; I'm not going to spell out what to look for."

"Understood." This was a test. Cat was determined to pass it.

"And you do it from behind the curtain, so you don't attract too much attention to yourself." Ms. Pryce emphasized her instruction by pointing at the exact spot Cat should position herself at.

Cat nodded and started to walk toward the curtain.

"If anyone approaches you, you refer them to Jeremy or myself, you understand?"

"Yes, ma'am," Cat mumbled under her breath.

It wasn't a glamorous job, but at least she was here in the midst of all the action. For that, Cat was immensely grateful. She found herself a chair and placed it just so that she could look out through a gap in the curtain without being seen by the crowd which had just started to pour in. The only other people back here with her were the warehouse staff responsible for moving high value lots on and off the stage.

The auction turnout was quite diverse; most of the people entering the room had dressed up for the occasion.

Men wore suits and women wore dresses and ensembles that wouldn't look out of place on the Duchess of Cambridge. Then there were those who stood out a bit more; Cat spied ethnic clothes of all colors and descriptions, and also some people who seemingly didn't care at all what they wore. Apparently the latter seemed to think that jeans and t-shirts were an appropriate fashion choice for an event such as this.

Cat idly wondered what Ms. Pryce would have to say about those people.

Finally, as the seats in front of the podium began to fill up, someone walked in who made Cat's heart stop.

Alexander.

On his arm was a slender, elegantly dressed woman with strawberry blond hair. Her features and skin tone reminded Cat of a porcelain doll, similar to the type her grandmother used to collect when she was still alive. A pang of jealousy surged through Cat's chest. Fine, she'd left in a hurry that night, and ruined any chance she'd had with the man. But here he was with another woman by his side, and Cat could barely contain her rage.

This makes no sense!

Cat took a deep breath and tried to focus on the clipboard in her lap. With this unexpected arrival, Cat's job was going to become so much more difficult. How could she observe the entire crowd, when all her eyes seemed to want to do was stare at one particular person?

She looked up to see where he'd sat down, and found

that he was looking right in her direction. Could he see her? That was impossible, surely! She was well hidden behind this curtain.

Cat blinked and saw that he'd looked away, making small talk with his female companion.

Ugh, what a player!

Just outside of Cat's range of view, someone—presumably the auctioneer—made a knocking sound.

"Ladies and gentlemen! Welcome to Sotheby's. You are here by invitation, since you are all valued clients of ours, so I think we can forego any explanations at this point. You all know how this works. We have an amazing selection of paintings, furniture, and numerous other objets d'art for you tonight. Without further ado, let's begin!"

Cat took a deep breath. This was it. She couldn't afford to miss a moment of it.

In a rush, she scribbled down the first lot number just as the auctioneer introduced it, and started scanning the crowd, pausing every time she hit the third row from the front, fourth person from the left. Alexander. Seeing him here brought back all sorts of memories she'd been trying to block.

He had a certain aura, a presence that was impossible to ignore. All the regret she'd done her best to swallow came rushing back. If she hadn't left in such a rush, and their encounter had come to a more logical end, would he have remembered her? Did he remember her now?

Perhaps she ought to find him later and say hello.

Then again, he was here with somebody. If she approached him, that would just be sad on her part.

She rubbed the bridge of her nose with the back of her pen and did her best to focus on the crowd again. Bidders 54 and 87 seemed to have a bit of a competition going. She noted down everything she saw, including the remark "this is personal."

The next lots passed in much the same fashion. Cat did her best to control the urge to let her gaze linger on Alexander, who had stayed out of the bidding so far, even if the shock of seeing him again refused to subside. And she wrote down whatever she could about the active bidders, just like Ms. Pryce had told her to. Before she knew it, she'd filled sheet after sheet in scribbles.

Her hand started to cramp—it had been an age since she'd written this much by hand—but she didn't miss a beat. Every lot, every bidder was carefully documented.

An hour had passed, and the auction was coming to an end. From her earlier study of the catalog, she knew that there was only one lot left.

And Alexander hadn't bid on a single item yet.

"Next up, lot 66, mounted prints from an unknown book, circa 1500, let's start with the reserve—" Cat heard the auctioneer say.

In the crowd, Alexander seemed to perk up in his chair. That was when Cat noticed the chair next to him was empty.

Cat held her breath and gripped the pen so tightly her knuckles turned white. The ache in her wrist that had started to develop soon after the auction had begun had now turned to shooting pains going all the way up through her arm and shoulder. For but a moment, Alexander seemed to look in her direction again and she thought she could see it. The passion, the care with which he'd looked at her that night. It was like a stab in the heart, forcing her to avert her gaze and focus on his hands instead.

Within moments, the bidding was underway. No matter who else lifted their paddle, almost a split second later, Alexander had his in the air. He was determined.

Cat wondered what made this lot so special. Sure, she'd been fascinated by its description herself, but Alexander seemed willing to spend a fortune on it. The higher the bids went, the more intrigued she became.

At the same time, a sense of great urgency filled her; this was the last lot. Once the auction ended, he would leave. The prospect hurt more than she expected it to.

By the end, a few framed bits of old paper had gone for five times their reserve. With her heart still hammering away and a lump developing in her throat, Cat looked down to find that she had unknowingly filled an entire page with just observations about Alexander. Most had nothing to do with the auction. Damn. No way could she show all this to Ms. Pryce; she would think Cat had lost her mind.

The auctioneer ended with some sort of announcement

about payments. Cat didn't waste any more time and sprang into action. She had to see what was so special about that lot Alexander had bought. If only to feel some sort of closeness to him, to understand what made him tick.

After catching a final glimpse of him, she headed deeper backstage to intercept that final lot on its way back into storage.

CHAPTER ELEVEN

Of course Alexander had known Catherine was there in the crowd somewhere from the moment he walked in. His sense of smell had never let him down before, and he'd recognize her special scent anywhere.

Sure enough, he'd pinpointed her as soon as he sat down; she was right behind the curtain. He could even make out those pale green eyes of hers, looking back at him from the dark.

He ought to feel triumphant; he'd finally achieved his goal of tracking her down. But as much as it pained him, he couldn't act on it. He couldn't afford to tip off Lucille, who for now seemed completely unaware of how close she was to giving Julius what, or who, he wanted.

They'd ended up at the auction together not as a bonding exercise between siblings, no. This was an unfortunate coincidence. It was his first auction in months and he had a clear goal: to obtain that very special item he'd found in the catalog.

Lucille was here because—well, he wasn't quite sure why. *Just looking for a bargain*, she'd said, which was odd, since Lucille didn't normally attend these types of events. Unsurprisingly, she hadn't bid on a single lot all night. And toward the end of the auction, she looked bored.

"All this old tat, who needs it?" she grumbled.

Alexander looked up from the catalog—only one lot remained until it was time for him to get in on the action. "It's almost over. If you don't see anything you fancy, why don't you head into the other room for some refreshments? I'll be right out after this," Alexander suggested.

They shared a look. He hadn't meant the actual snacks and champagne next door, and she knew it.

"Very well. I don't know why you'd want to stay until the end anyway," Lucille said as she got up from her chair and elegantly navigated through the row of chairs toward the exit, attracting curious looks as she went.

Alexander smiled to himself. This was her hunting technique. Lucille knew exactly how to use her talents to get what she wanted.

She glanced down at a middle aged, slightly balding man at the end of the row and shot him a subtle smile. The man, confused for a second, regained his composure and got up as well, following Lucille out into the next room.

Alexander shook his head. *There goes another poor sod.* Luckily for him, vampires didn't kill anymore, not for centuries, ever since the Council became established and laid down the rules in the Treaty of London, 1789.

No, he'd be fine, eventually. At most he'd feel hungover, and wonder what might have happened in the inevitable gap Lucille would leave in his memory.

With Lucille out of the room, Alexander could relax a

little bit and focus on the task at hand. He had to get his hands on that final lot: what he presumed to be some missing pages from the *Encyclopedia of Myth and Magick*. The more he'd thought about it, the more certain he'd been. The illustrations and lettering were too similar for it to be a coincidence.

Perhaps they'd contain nothing of use, perhaps they'd change his whole understanding of the situation with Catherine. Either way, he wanted them for his library. It was a matter of pride. And knowing that Catherine was here somewhere just strengthened his resolve further. It had to be a sign.

The bidding was furious; clearly he wasn't the only one interested in some tattered pieces of paper from an old book most people would probably reject as pure fiction. But he knew better than that. And in the end, he was victorious.

Who says money can't buy happiness, he thought with a wry grin on his face.

If only everything else was equally simple.

The auction was over, and the crowd started to leave. Only those with winning bids stayed behind to complete the necessary formalities. Alexander paid by check; he'd never gotten used to electronic transactions. The feel of the booklet in his hand, the sound of the perforated paper tearing—those little things made a purchase feel real in a way that making a phone call to a banker or pushing a piece of plastic into a machine could never do.

As the young woman accepted his check and completed the necessary paperwork, Alexander grew increasingly restless. Catherine was here somewhere. As was Lucille.

He wanted nothing more than to find and speak to her. Even if Catherine wanted nothing more to do with him, he yearned to be in her presence again.

But if Lucille found out... That would be a disaster.

He couldn't risk it. So as he waited for the receipt, he impatiently tapped his foot and scanned the room for any sign of his sister. She had to be done with that man by now. Had she caught Catherine's scent as well?

While he stood here to finalize his shopping, disaster could be unfolding somewhere behind the scenes.

Just as the woman behind the counter handed him his newly printed bill, he felt a presence right behind him.

"What did you buy?" Lucille asked.

Alexander folded the paper in half, then again in half and put it into the inner pocket of his jacket.

"Just some prints," he said, smiling at Lucille to cover his nerves.

The latter squinted suspiciously. "Prints?"

It wasn't a lie, technically. The pages had been printed, and mounted as though they were in fact works of art. Alexander nodded and smiled again. "I think they'll go very nicely in the library."

"How much art does one man need?" Lucille scoffed.

At least she seemed satisfied for now; she was still

licking her lips after her earlier human snack.

"How were the refreshments?" Alexander steered the conversation away from his purchase.

Lucille sighed. "Oh, quite satisfactory. I was hungrier than I thought."

Alexander chuckled. "It was written all over your face."

Lucille placed her arm inside the crook of his as they walked toward the exit. With every passing step, he felt Catherine's presence less keenly. Alexander turned around one last time just as they passed through the set of double doors into the reception hall. He didn't know what to feel: relief or heartache.

It turned out to be a heavy dose of both.

"Anything wrong?" Lucille asked.

Alexander shook his head. "No, all fine. I think I might have overpaid for those prints."

Lucille laughed. "Swept up in auction fever. With the years of practice you've had, I thought you'd be better than that."

Alexander shrugged. "It can happen to the best of us."

As they walked through the crowds of humans on the way out, more than a few heads turned in their direction. Men, as well as women. Such was the attraction of the vampire. Some humans were drawn to them like moths who had no idea how close they came to being burned to death.

Nobody ever sensed the danger until it was too late. Except Catherine. She'd figured it out. Sadly, her keen sense of observation might have plunged her into more danger than she could imagine.

"Now what?" Alexander asked.

He hoped she would go her own way, so that he could do the same. What if she wanted to linger, though? What if Catherine walked in here to join the crowds of auction-goers, and Lucille picked up her scent? Then what?

Could Alexander choose Catherine over his sister? He'd try his best to avoid that scenario. But if it came down to it, he supposed that he could.

"Council work, you know." Lucille brushed away his question.

Alexander nodded. With a bit of luck, he wouldn't have to make that difficult choice. Not today.

"I'll walk with you," Alexander suggested.

Lucille agreed with a nod as they passed into the darkness outside.

"How goes the hunt?" he asked, once they were out of earshot of the other humans leaving the auction house.

She shrugged. "Nobody seems to know this woman."

"Yes, I noticed the same," Alexander said.

"But our dear maker isn't one to give up easy, as you well know."

"Julius is a great many things, but he's not a quitter," Alexander said bitterly. And therein lay the problem.

They walked on in silence, further and further away from Catherine's last known location. How glad he was that he'd been able to avoid any confrontation at the auction.

Alexander didn't even notice how far they'd walked when they came to a stop in front of a rundown building somewhere in the middle of Chinatown.

"Well, this is me," Lucille said.

Alexander glanced up at the unassuming façade. Humans would walk by here and ignore this place, but he knew better. It was one of the bigger lodging houses for young vampires; in the olden days, one might have called it a coven house.

"I thought you had better taste than this, sister," Alexander remarked.

Lucille let out a chuckle. "I don't live here, silly! Just doing the rounds, making inquiries... Perhaps someone in here has come across that woman. Perhaps I can convince some of them to join the search."

Alexander looked up at the boarded up windows on the upper floors. There was no way of knowing how many newly turned immortals lurked behind these walls. The Council truly had an army at their disposal.

He shrugged. "Well, best of luck in your efforts. I'll head back myself."

"I'll see you around," Lucille said.

Her tone was innocuous, but to Alexander's ears, her goodbye had sounded more like a threat.

"Yes, see you," he responded.

As he turned, he heard Lucille's footsteps climb up the front steps to enter the building. He started walking leisurely, but as soon as he turned the corner, he broke into a sprint. What were the chances of Catherine still being there, at Sotheby's?

Slim, probably. Still, he owed it to her as well as himself to try to intercept her.

CHAPTER TWELVE

Cat couldn't believe what she'd just seen.

Even after the warehouse workers had taken the final lot of tonight's auction away, Cat still stood frozen in place, right in front of the heavy duty elevator.

Although they were hard to read, some of the passages on those framed pages had been pretty damning. They mentioned the so-called undead. Vampires. There were even illustrations to go with the text that looked unlike anything she'd seen before.

She didn't believe in stuff like that, or did she?

Cat remembered the old portrait that seemed to feature Alexander. That could have been a funny coincidence, or a very clever reproduction piece that looked a lot older than it really was.

She recalled the dream she had of him later that very night; the details of what exactly happened had been fuzzy, unclear, but it all came to her as soon as she read those pages. Somehow, her subconscious had already figured out what he was. Then there were those two funny marks she'd seen on Shelly's neck. Had she just imagined all of this stuff?

Her mind tried to rationalize everything, to convince her that the supernatural didn't exist, even if all the evidence pointed toward it.

And he'd been here. He'd bought this very item without bidding on anything else, which could potentially explain everything! Was that a coincidence too?

All around, people were rushing back and forth, finishing up for the night. Cat forced herself into action to do the same.

She grabbed the clipboard with her notes, as well as her handbag, and made a beeline for the exit. At home, she'd talk to Shelly and realize that probably she was just stressed out and all of it was messing with her head. Yes, that had to be it. Better sense had to prevail.

Nobody seemed to pay much attention to her as she left. Even the streets were unusually quiet on her way.

Still, once she found herself in a near-empty tube station, waiting for the next train, she couldn't shake the feeling that she was being watched.

Again.

She'd felt the same after her first day last week, when Shelly had dragged her to the pub.

Perhaps this was what it felt like to lose your mind?

Cat wrapped her arms around her handbag tightly and scanned the platform. Of the few people around, most didn't seem to be looking at her at all. An old couple stared intently at the board announcing the next train. A man in a business suit was tapping away at his phone. Further up, there was a man in tattered jeans and an old, faded canvas jacket, who rummaged around in one of the two large plastic bags he'd been carrying earlier.

All of them were way too busy to be paying attention to Cat.

And yet...

A gust of wind blew across the platform, adding to the eerie atmosphere. *It'll be an approaching train*, Cat tried to reassure herself. Her hands went numb in the cold so she pushed them deeper into her pockets.

After an unseasonably warm October, winter had finally come.

Or perhaps it wasn't the weather that made her feel cold. A chill slowly crawled down her back, causing her to turn around and scan the other side of the platform again. *Nothing. Nobody.*

She closed her eyes and slowly counted down from ten—an old relaxation trick her mom had taught her when she was little and still afraid of the dark.

When she opened her eyes, she saw the lights of the approaching train. Finally. She'd be safe in there, and it would take her straight home.

Cat raced at the nearest door and sat down in one of the many empty seats. The train was quiet as well, but brightly lit and a lot less scary than the station had been. There was a surveillance camera on the ceiling, aimed squarely at Cat, reassuring her further. If anyone tried anything, they'd be caught on film.

She folded her arms and kept her eyes fixed on the platform. Only those few people who had been waiting earlier made it into the train. Nobody looked out of place or dangerous in any way.

The doors closed, allowing her to breathe another sigh of relief. She'd made it. The train pulled away, slowly at first, then speeding up through the dark.

Cat rested her hand on her chest and felt her heartbeat slow down back to normal again. She slumped against the back rest of her seat and closed her eyes.

Alexander smiled at her, and she smiled back.

———◆———

When Cat came back to her senses, she was no longer on the train. The street she found herself on didn't look familiar.

This wasn't her neighborhood. Had she been sleepwalking? To make matters worse, it had begun to drizzle; her hair was already damp.

She had no clue where she was going, and yet her feet kept moving of their own accord.

House upon house passed her by, each one grander and more luxurious than the last.

Finally, she stood in front of a large ornamental gate and it hit her.

She was on Kensington Palace Gardens.

This was Alexander's villa!

She wanted to turn around and run, but something gave her pause. All those dreams she'd had of Alexander were hard to ignore. The closer she got to the gate, the safer she felt somehow. At the same time, the feeling of unease she'd felt at the metro station earlier was creeping up to her again. Something dangerous lurked in the darkness behind her, she was sure of it. She shivered as the damp crept through her coat.

Where her instincts had told her to run from this place on Halloween, today they were screaming the opposite. *Go in. He'll protect you.*

It made no sense. Why would he want anything to do with her, after the way she left things that night?

The gates opened of their own accord, and she stepped inside. It didn't matter that the more rational voice in her head insisted she had no business here. That he wouldn't want to see her anyway. That he was probably in there with the woman who had accompanied him to Sotheby's. Pangs of jealousy tore at her heart.

Yet her heart insisted she had to proceed.

She turned around one last time as the gates shut slowly behind her. There was something there, across the road. Two eyes, glowing red, staring right back at her. Her heart skipped a few beats and she swallowed, hard.

Cat clutched her handbag tightly with both hands and ran up the driveway toward the house. The gravel shifted and crunched under her feet, making it near impossible to maintain her balance on her heels. She stumbled and almost fell as she reached the front steps.

One of the two large wooden doors opened and a familiar silhouette appeared in front of her.

"Catherine!" Alexander called out.

Within the blink of an eye, he stood in front of her, at the bottom of the steps. How had he moved so quickly?

"Catherine. You came," he spoke again.

Cat didn't know how to respond. She blinked a few times, almost expecting him to vanish right before her eyes. Maybe she'd fallen asleep on the train, and this was all a crazy dream?

"Someone is following me," Cat mumbled, taking a shaky step forward. Her knees trembled, and almost straightaway, so did the rest of her.

"I'll protect you," he said as he reached out for her arm, steadying her.

Somehow, she believed him.

This was crazy and completely impossible. She took a step and promptly lost her balance again. He caught her. At once, she felt weightless; they didn't walk up the steps together, they floated. All she could focus on was his hand on her arm, burning through her damp clothes and setting her heart alight.

Dream or not, if she assumed that everything she'd learned was true, and he was a vampire, did it really matter? This right here, it felt right. She'd be a lot safer inside the house with him, than with whatever was out there watching her.

As soon as they crossed the threshold into his house, she froze. There it was, the painting that had started everything and almost ended it too.

She'd been captivated by it before she'd even met the

man himself.

The door shut behind them with a loud click and the outside world seemed to no longer matter.

"You'll have questions." Alexander turned to face her. His expression was soft, almost gentle, even if the flicker in his eyes suggested something more. Was it passion that she saw? Her body's reaction to him was obvious; the elevated heart rate, butterflies in her stomach, all of it hit her like a freight train, and threatened to throw her off balance again.

"I'm not sure I want to know the answers," Cat mumbled.

She glanced down at her shoes, which were scuffed and coated in streaks of mud. Her one good pair of heels.

Cat met his gaze again and his dark eyes lit up. He didn't scare her anymore. Something about him invited her to proceed. Just like on that first night, before everything had gone wrong. Her mind went blank except for one thought: how good it had felt to kiss him.

She tiptoed and let her desires take over. Before she knew it, his arms were wrapped around her, and his lips had locked with hers. It was familiar, like they'd done this so many times before; of course in a way they had, in her dreams. Soft lips, begging for affection, their tongues twirling and darting around one another in an endless game of cat and mouse.

Cat felt feverish, overcome with sensations. This one kiss seemed to unleash all the tension and yearning she'd felt for weeks.

"I'm sorry," she whispered, in between kisses.

He didn't stop or respond. How was it that he still wanted *her*, when he surrounded himself with women such as the one who had accompanied him to the auction?

The more she drank in his essence, the less important her questions seemed. The only thing that mattered was that she was here, with him. And that he wanted her back.

Cat stumbled backward, her knees buckling underneath her. Their lips disconnected, though his muscular arms still cradled her. For a moment, she had trouble identifying her surroundings, then her eyes settled on the hunting scene on the wall next to them.

"That painting." Cat nodded at the canvas.

"That's me. Yes," Alexander confirmed, like he'd read her mind.

A sense of déjà vu came over Cat. He'd had his arms around her when she asked him this in her dream. She recalled what came next: a dance and a bite to the neck. Had it really been a dream, or a bizarre vision of the future? Her heart started to race again, but she felt more excited than scared this time.

"You are a..." She paused, unable to say the word out loud. *Vampire.*

It still seemed so crazy, so impossible. Everything was going so well; despite everything, he really seemed to be into her. She wasn't ready to slip up and make a fool of herself.

Alexander smiled and brushed a wet lock of hair out of her face. "Let's get you cleaned up. You must be freezing."

He was right; in all the excitement she'd forgotten just how sorry a state she was in. Cat nodded and slipped her arm into his. Halfway up the stairs, something changed. A fresh dose of dread came over her, causing her chest to constrict and heart to pound even harder. She stopped and scanned the hall, then paused when she saw a man staring up at her. His eyes shone deep red. *Danger.*

"There's someone there," she whispered.

Alexander paused as well. "That's just Michael. He won't harm you."

Cat frowned and bit her lip. Her instincts were trying to tell her otherwise, and yet she was inclined to believe Alexander's reassurances. He would protect her, no matter what.

"You're safe, I promise," he said.

Downstairs, there was no sign of the other man anymore, and instantly, her fear subsided.

CHAPTER THIRTEEN

Alexander could hardly believe it. After he'd returned to Sotheby's and found no sign of her, he'd come home defeated. And now, it was Catherine who had come to him.

She'd kissed him with a need that seemed to match, if not surpass his own.

Only now, her eyes were wide and fearful again. He wanted so badly to reassure her, to convince her that she had nothing to fear from him.

Was that the truth, though? As he found himself so close to her, with her scent overwhelming his senses once more, could he honestly say that she wasn't in danger?

The temptation was stronger than the last time. Every fiber in his body seemed to scream at him to go for her throat, as well as her lips.

He realized it had been days since he'd last fed; all his energy these days had gone into trying to track her down.

"You're safe," he heard himself say.

It felt like a hollow promise, even if he really wanted to believe it himself. The way Michael had looked at her from the bottom of the stairs had suggested he too had fallen under the spell of the Blood Bride. Even if his loyalty to Alexander prevented him from acting on it, and Alexander somehow managed to suppress his own urges, they still had the Council to deal with. No doubt it was one of theirs who had followed Cat here in the first place.

He glanced at her as they continued up the steps and through the hallway, a journey they'd made together before. Their destination was the same too: the master suite. Once again, his eloquence was failing him; he wasn't sure how to talk to her, especially while she looked so vulnerable.

"I know this is a lot to take in," Alexander said finally.

She didn't respond, just looked up at him, and he was overcome with desire. He ached to kiss her, hold her, and comfort her.

But despite their earlier affections, it would be selfish of him to give in. This wasn't the time. Catherine was shivering visibly now. Humans were sensitive creatures, susceptible to all sorts of dangers. The last thing he wanted was for her to catch a cold on top of everything.

"The en-suite is through there." Alexander pointed at a door leading off from the other side of the bedroom. "You'll find a robe there if you want it."

He turned and walked back out of the room to give her some privacy.

"Don't go," Catherine whispered behind him. "Please."

He stopped. For her sake as well as his own, he should probably leave. But he couldn't deny her request either.

So he did as asked, closed the door behind him, and sat down on a chair in the corner with his hands folded. Within moments, he heard the sound of the shower inside the en-suite. He tried not to imagine her in there, warm water rushing down her curves, caressing her and soothing her.

There was no way of knowing how much time they had together before Lucille would inevitably interrupt. Michael would protect them, but he was their only ally against who knew how many Council loyalists? He could only hope that the safeguards this house offered would keep them out long enough.

It was obvious what they had to do. He'd seen the ritual performed once before, many years ago. Alexander rested his head in his hands.

Catherine's sense of reality was already shattered. Although his own initiation into this world had taken place several hundred years ago, he could clearly remember how frazzled he'd been. This wasn't an easy truth to be faced with.

The click of the bathroom door snapped him out of his thoughts. There she stood in the doorway, wearing his black robe. Clouds of steam billowed around her, carrying the scents of a summer meadow in full bloom into the room with it.

A radiant image of womanhood, her expression was calmer now. Perhaps she was coming to terms with where she'd ended up? He didn't know what to say, how to broach the subject.

"There is something about you," Catherine started.

Alexander's ears perked up. That meant she had felt it

too, the inexplicable connection they shared.

"I've dreamed a lot about you," she spoke, as though she could read his mind. This very image, in fact, of Catherine fresh out of the shower, had visited him in his sleep before.

"Yes." Alexander got up and approached her while maintaining eye contact. The sweet smell of her blood was even more intense now that she had warmed up. How easy it would be to hypnotize her, to make her bend to his will right now. And how hollow a victory it would be.

"And you make me feel safe," she continued.

"I want you to feel safe." He meant it, and yet it felt like a lie.

Catherine raised her hand. "I'm not done yet."

Alexander paused.

"But at the same time, there's something in this house that makes me feel otherwise. Maybe your man, Michael." Catherine shuddered as she spoke his name. "Maybe something else." She frowned, like she was surprised at her own words.

Alexander took another step in her direction. This was his opening, his chance to explain the entire wretched situation to her. If she ran again, at least it would be after she had all the facts. "There is something you need to know."

Catherine averted her gaze and wrapped her arms around herself tightly.

"You're not like other women."

Her eyes snapped back up at his again and she raised an eyebrow.

"I'm not saying this to flatter you, I'm stating a fact. Perhaps you've noticed it before." Alexander ran his hand through his hair as he tried to find the right words to continue.

"Our kind—" He paused and rested his gaze on her lips.

"Vampires," she whispered.

He nodded. It was good to hear her say it finally.

"You'll know the stories. The immortality, the drinking of blood. But we're not murderers." He started pacing around the room as he spoke.

"No?"

He shook his head. "It's against the law. We feed just enough to sustain ourselves, but we're not allowed to harm humans. Not that I personally would ever want to even if it were allowed. We're not monsters. Most of us aren't, anyway." He was rambling. This wasn't good. He paused for a moment to see how she was taking all the information so far.

"Then why do I keep feeling like I've got death hanging over my head?" Catherine said.

"Because you do. You're different, as I said."

She walked up to the bed and sat down in the center of it. Then she looked back up at him.

"Your blood is special. Any vampire who gets close to you falls under your spell. That's why you're being stalked."

He stopped and looked down at her.

"So there are vampires after me for my blood?" Her eyes widened again, and her bottom lip trembled slightly.

So fragile, so beautiful. How could she not know the power she wielded?

"Unfortunately, in your particular case, the laws mean next to nothing. They'll drink every last drop of it, no matter the consequences."

"Except you. You don't want to... kill me?" she whispered.

Alexander shook his head.

"And that's why I feel safe with you, but not any of the others?" she asked.

Alexander ran his hand over his chin. Her conclusion was logical. He started pacing back and forth again.

"It's only a matter of time before they find you here. Whoever was out there was probably tracking you on their behalf." It hurt to admit it, but it was the truth and she deserved to know. "I'll do everything I can to keep you safe. But we are outnumbered."

"I trust you." She looked up at him, and he found himself lost in the depths of her green eyes and froze.

It was bittersweet, hearing her say those three little words. He was unworthy. Throughout their interactions, he'd been teetering on the edge of control. Even as they kissed, he was only a hair's breadth away from satisfying his intense thirst. The slightest misstep, and his dark side would destroy everything they had.

"Why?" he asked finally.

She blinked a few times and frowned. "I can't explain. It's what's in my heart."

"Maybe it's a sign," Alexander mumbled.

"What?" she asked.

He shook his head. All of this was highly illogical. Their connection, as well as the fact that he could resist her—at least for now. He might as well throw all logic out the window and follow his heart too. There was only one way out; he had to take a chance. A leap of faith.

So he walked up to her until he was only a step away from the bed. Then he fell down onto one knee and reached out for her right hand. A surge of electricity seemed to pass from her hand into his, so intense was the sensation of touching her again.

"I know this makes no sense, but I must ask. Knowing everything you do now, and considering what your heart is telling you... Would you walk the earth with me, companions in life and death, now and forever?"

"Are you... Is this a proposal?" she stammered and drew her hand back a little, though not far enough to break their connection.

Of course she was taken aback. They hardly knew each other beyond what their instincts were trying to tell them. In these modern times, they didn't make commitments anymore until much later on in relationships. He had let his old fashioned ideas get out of control and jumped the gun.

Alexander averted his gaze and was about to get up again when she placed her other hand on his arm.

"Wait. I need to know your reasons."

When he raised his head and saw how she looked at him, with those expressive eyes, overflowing with emotion, he knew that perhaps, there was hope still. He just had to work for it. Alexander closed his eyes to collect his thoughts.

"Because from the moment I saw you, you shone a light into the darkest crevices of my heart. You reminded me of what it's like to be alive. You make me feel things I haven't felt in over three hundred years." He opened his eyes again as he spoke, noting the surprise on Catherine's face at his last statement.

Of course, she knew about him only in theory, but learning how long he'd lived in his current form really seemed to hit home.

"Three hundred years? That's how old you are?" Catherine whispered.

Alexander nodded. Thereabouts.

"And in all that time, you never thought to settle down?"

"Never crossed my mind." It was the truth. Even in life, he never married, which had greatly frustrated his parents when they were still alive.

"Wow."

CHAPTER FOURTEEN

Cat didn't know whether to laugh or cry. She was in so much turmoil that her brain had trouble catching up. This wasn't a casual question, or an impulsive move on his part. He had waited for centuries for the right person. The commitment he asked of her was permanent—she could feel it. They couldn't just change their minds and get a divorce like normal people did.

What made *her* so special? Just her blood? No, then he would have simply fed on her and cast her aside.

Alexander looked up at her from his kneeling position with his hand still holding on to hers. Every time she looked into his eyes, her feelings for him deepened. He expected an answer; she couldn't drag this on endlessly.

Could she live with him and love him forever? A man she barely knew? Her heart said yes. In matters of love, it was the heart you really had to listen to, not the mind, right?

"You'll have to give up a lot," Alexander spoke softly. "I won't sugarcoat it."

Cat waited for him to continue, even though she wasn't sure anything he was about to say would sway her. Her decision wasn't based on rationality after all.

"Once it's done, you'll live here," Alexander said.

She looked around the opulent room. That didn't seem

like much of a sacrifice.

"You'll never be able to tell your family or friends about the true nature of our relationship. My powers ensure that you won't age like other humans, so when the time comes that your enduring youth will raise suspicions, you'll have to cut ties with everyone you know from your previous life."

Cat swallowed hard. She'd have to say goodbye to Shelly, to her mom as well as her brothers. Then again, if she lived forever and they didn't, she'd have to say goodbye to them eventually anyway.

"And then there is the matter of the Council." Alexander's voice turned grim.

"The Council?"

"The other vampires that are after you. By law, they're not permitted to harm you if we proceed, but they'll be furious." He paused for a moment. "Of course, I'll do my best to keep you safe no matter what you decide."

"If they're not allowed to harm me, so what if they're angry." Cat shrugged.

She knew what she had to do. Despite everything he'd told her, it still felt right.

"Ask me again," she whispered.

He did. She said yes.

What happened next was a blur. Alexander, with tears of joy in his eyes, got up and swept her up into his arms. She didn't resist; there was no need to. They kissed again, and as intense as her feelings for him had been before, they were even stronger now.

Before she knew it, he had her on the bed and crawled on top of her and assaulted her whole upper body with his lips. His movements were so fast, she had a hard time focusing, and only felt the touch of his lips after he had moved on to the next spot.

The entire experience was like a dream. Like she only had to think about where she wanted him to kiss her next, and he'd already done it.

At the same time, her hands roamed his body. His beautiful, flawless body. What she felt through his crisp white shirt perfectly matched many a naughty dream. How could it be that her imagination had got everything so spot on?

She reached out for the buttons on his shirt, attempting to open them one by one. He wasn't so patient, and tore it off in one swift move. He did the same to her robe, leaving it in tatters on the floor.

He had a wild streak in him—of course he did. He had the potential of being a dangerous predator, an animal, with urges and instincts that went deeper than any human could ever feel. Catherine had put her life in his hands. Seeing just a glimpse of what he was capable of took her breath away.

"I'm sorry, I didn't mean to scare you," he said.

"You didn't," she gasped. "Don't stop!"

Before she'd even finished her demand, he'd flipped her onto her stomach and started his assault on her back.

Kisses and nibbles all the way down her spine. He ran his hands over her curves, tickling her with his fingertips, before reaching down between her legs.

"You're wet," he growled.

She could only moan in response. His fingers knew how to play her, like an expert pianist would his favorite instrument. She wasn't a virgin, though she wasn't as experienced as Shelly was. Still, Cat was certain even Shelly had never had an intimate encounter quite like this one.

"I've dreamed of this," he whispered, as he entered her with two fingers, sending her lower abdomen into a spasm of lust.

So have I, Cat thought, but she was unable to form the words.

Behind her, the sound of further tearing fabric suggested he was ready to take things to the next level. Cat tried to raise herself up onto her elbows, perhaps catch a glimpse of him behind her. He didn't wait for her to complete the maneuver, just flipped her again, spread her legs, and dove down into her sweet folds for a taste of her essence.

She squealed and bucked her hips up into his face, savoring the feeling of his tongue buried deep inside of her. He was so good at this. Those hundreds of years of experience sure as hell paid off right now.

A strange sensation came over her, a tightening of all her muscles at once, a sweet tickle that started at the point where his tongue had just been and extended all the way through her womb.

Alexander pulled back, leaving her aching for more.

"No!" she cried out, clawing at his shoulders in an attempt to push him back down.

He straightened himself and entered her in the traditional fashion instead.

Never before had missionary felt so good. She reached out for him and wrapped her arms and legs around him tightly. His solid muscle pressed into her generous curves. They fit together like a glove.

As she ran her hands over his back, she could feel his power: muscles contracting and releasing, thrusting into her with a level of control and speed she'd never encountered before.

This entire exercise seemed effortless, such was his power and strength. While she was out of breath and coated in a thin layer of sweat already, he seemed to have endless reserves of energy to draw from.

Could she ever satisfy him the way he fulfilled *her* every need? Cat looked up at him, focusing on his eyes, which told her everything she needed to know.

Her being here with him—surrendering to him—was all he needed.

She stifled a cry, which then involuntarily turned into a scream.

"Oh, God!"

Her body did the rest, releasing a flood of endorphins into her bloodstream as her lower abdomen spasmed. Out of breath, and out of words, she lay on her back, gasping for air as her orgasm continued to wash over her in waves.

Alexander gathered her up in his arms and thrust into her one final time before erupting himself and filling her with his seed. He lowered himself onto her, his face resting on her chest until her breaths started to calm.

"That was amazing," Cat whispered.

He didn't respond, just raised his head to give her a peck on the lips. Only then could she see what toll their activities had taken on him.

"You look tired. I didn't realize vampires could look tired," she said, while running her hand through his hair.

"Not tired, just hungry," he mumbled, then gave in to her embrace once more.

Hungry? She was about to say something stupid about going down to the kitchen and fixing him a snack when she realized what he meant.

"Do you want to... you know?" She straightened her neck and gestured at it.

He shook his head. "Not yet. Not until it's official."

She kept caressing his hair while they rested. The only sounds cutting through the silence were her own breaths and the soft ticking of a clock.

"How long do you think we have?" she wondered aloud. If someone had followed her here, it wouldn't be long until they called in the so-called Council and turned up with reinforcements. "Before those people who are after me turn up?"

"They'll be here before the night is over. My security measures will keep them out for a while..." Alexander stretched and leaned up on his elbow.

The short rest had made all the difference; he looked reinvigorated. Flawless, like before.

"It's important we perform the ritual before they make it inside. Are you ready?" he asked.

Cat bit her lip. The moment of truth.

"Yes," she whispered. It was crazy to think about all that had happened in such a short period of time. But this wasn't the time for reflection, it was the time to act.

Cat took a deep breath and forced a smile.

"Yes. I am ready," she repeated, with more confidence this time.

"I'll get Michael to prepare the library." Alexander's expression was solemn. No doubt this was a big step even for him.

Cat nodded and watched as Alexander got up. What a sight. She glanced down at her own naked body, then at the torn robe on the floor.

"There's a selection of things in the wardrobe," Alexander said. "Something is bound to fit."

It was like the man could read her mind.

———— ◆ ————

Barely half an hour had passed before Cat found herself next to a make-shift altar in the library, with Alexander by her side.

The other vampire, Michael, had agreed to stand guard outside in case trouble arrived. They'd have no witnesses, but apparently the ritual would be valid nonetheless.

"It's not difficult, or lengthy, but it's important we follow all the steps until the end." Alexander pointed at the numbered list in the ancient text that lay on the table next to them.

Cat nodded. She wanted to do it right, and not just because their safety depended on it.

"First, we create our bond, then we ask the questions. I'll begin." Alexander picked up the small dagger that was incorporated into the spine of the book and held it up to the index finger on his right hand. He cut himself, not too deep, just enough for a single deep red drop to form. Then he handed the dagger to Cat.

"You do the left," he said.

She hesitated for a moment. *This is the right thing to do.* She took a deep breath and pressed the sharp point of the dagger into her left index finger. Her blood flowed much more willingly, as though her body was as keen to complete the ritual as her heart had been.

They stood facing one another and held up their hands, pressing them together until the blood on their index fingers mingled into one. The realization that she was one step closer to finalizing her bond with Alexander made Cat's heart surge.

As she caught her breath, he retrieved a deep red ribbon that had so far served as a bookmark in the old manuscript, and handed her one end of it.

"This symbolizes that we will forever be connected," he whispered.

Together they placed the center of the ribbon between their index and middle finger, then started to wrap it around, threading it through their fingers and around their wrists, holding them together.

He smiled at her; she thought she could detect a hint of nerves in his expression. This was possibly as big a step for him as it was for her.

Now, it was time for the next step. The questions.

Alexander glanced over at the old book, then made eye contact with her again. Images of their earlier encounter filled her mind. Would they be like this forever?

"Will you swear on everyone you hold dear, that you, Catherine Knight, pledge yourself to me, in life and in death, now and forever?"

"They're here," a voice—Michael's—called out from the other side of the door. Sure enough, Cat could hear shouting and thumping noises, as though people were trying to break in. Her fight or flight response tried to kick in, but she suppressed the urge to flee. It didn't matter, anyway. They were on the last step and the intruders would be too late.

"I will." Her voice trembled as she spoke. "Will you, Alexander Broderick the Third, pledge yourself to me, in life and in death, now and forever?"

Her heart jumped when she saw a little change in

Alexander's eyes. The passion, the fire, it was all still there. But there was something else in there as well. Was it love? He barely knew her—how could he be so sure he'd want her forever?

"I will."

Cat and Alexander didn't stir; they still stood in the center of the library, their hands with the deep red ribbon still in place and their eyes locked on. As crazy as the past few hours had been, this was the right way forward; Cat had never been so sure of anything in her entire life.

This man—vampire—who stood before her was willing to sacrifice everything for her safety.

The ritual was done; she felt the change in her. The noise outside grew, and Alexander positioned himself square to the door, partially blocking her view of it.

CHAPTER FIFTEEN

Alexander stood tall, with his eyes fixed on the door leading into the library. The ruckus outside had grown in intensity; clearly the intruders were now right outside with only this one pane of wood separating them from him and Catherine, who stood by his side.

He glanced at her. Should he feel differently about her now? Their connection had been intense even before they made it official.

The doors swung open with a loud crash, and Catherine flinched backward. He joined her and tightened his grip on her hand.

"We'll be fine," he mumbled, though he wasn't quite certain of it himself.

"Alexander!" Julius bellowed as he marched in past what was left of the door. "Hand her over, right this instant!"

Alexander took a step to his right, positioning himself in front of Catherine. His gesture was more symbolic than anything. The sheer age difference between Julius and Alexander ensured that the former was much more powerful. If it came to an actual battle, Alexander knew he didn't stand a chance.

And worse still, Julius hadn't come alone. His position in the Council meant he had support, no matter what. Just behind Julius stood Lucille, of course, and Gillian, as well as a number of other vampires Alexander didn't know. Behind them, a disheveled and bruised Michael peeked inside with a concerned frown on his face.

But Catherine was too important for Alexander to simply give up. He would fight if he had to. From the start, he'd wanted to protect her, even if that meant going against his deepest, darkest instincts, which had wanted to experience the taste of her blood, just as every other vampire did.

"I will not." Alexander stared at Julius; the resolve was written all over his face.

"Then I will have no choice but to compel you, son." Julius balled his fists and stared back.

"I thought you said we'd be safe if we completed that ritual," Catherine whispered behind Alexander.

Looking at the determined expression on Julius' face, Alexander could offer no reassurances to comfort to her. Yes, technically she should have been safe. But all the signs seemed to suggest that Julius was in no mood to follow the rules. He wasn't used to having to face opposition. Ever since he'd taken his place at the head of the council, he had become used to his will ruling supreme.

"Julius, master," Lucille said, her voice gentle and calm, very unlike her usual demeanor.

"Yes, child. What is it?" Julius spoke quickly, impatiently.

"I see the change in her," Lucille said, her voice

growing even softer.

Alexander turned his head to look at Catherine. Sure enough, he saw it too. There was a special glow about her. Humans wouldn't see it, of course, but it was clear as day to all the vampires in the room.

"Oh, what nonsense!" Gillian protested from the back. "I don't see anything!"

"How dare you!" Julius roared. "I gave you everything, and you repay me by spitting in my face?"

"She is my wife. I knew it from the moment I first saw her, and not even you, the great Principis of the Council, can undo that!" Alexander responded.

Julius charged ahead and Alexander moved back into position, blocking Catherine from the incoming assault.

He braced for impact, but Julius stopped dead with only inches between them and his hand wrapped around Alexander's throat. His eyes, once rich with experience and wisdom collected over two millennia, now only expressed one thing: blind rage. If he chose to, his fingernails would dig into Alexander's flesh and rip out his esophagus. Although not fatal, the trauma would be enough to disable Alexander long enough that Julius would win the battle immediately.

Behind them, Catherine let out a choked sob, which tore at Alexander's heart. It had just been a few hours since she'd been initiated into this parallel world Alexander and his kind inhabited. And already, she had to deal with the threat of death or worse, at the hands of the most powerful vampire in the world. It was too much. He was responsible; if he hadn't thrown that party, none of this would have happened.

"Master," Lucille spoke again. "The laws are clear."

Julius' frustration was obvious. He waved his other hand dismissively in her direction. "I know, I know. The laws forbid me from harming her."

He turned and stared into Alexander's eyes again. "But nowhere is it written I should spare a subject who disobeyed clear orders." The grip on Alexander's throat tightened painfully.

Lucille cleared her throat.

"What?" Julius let go of Alexander and flung around.

"As I see it, in a way this boils down to a property dispute." Lucille averted her gaze from Julius and looked directly at Alexander now.

Hearing her refer to Catherine as mere property made Alexander's blood boil. But he didn't argue, hoping that whatever Lucille was about to say would help defuse the situation further. At least he was no longer subjected to Julius' death grip.

"How so?" Julius barked.

"Well, you claimed the Blood Bride as property of the Council. Alexander claimed her as his consort, a process that is known to begin upon a couple's first meeting. His bond is stronger, and should take precedence. Yet that doesn't change the fact that a debt is being owed here."

"Explain!"

Alexander balled his fists. If Lucille suggested he share Catherine with Julius, he was going to rip her head off along with everyone else's. Sister or no sister.

"Well, as per our laws, Alexander owes you a Blood Bride—any Blood Bride—and the debt will be repaid." Lucille bowed her head as a show of respect and awaited a response.

"You're not actually considering this ridiculous suggestion, are you?" Gillian's voice was shrill with anger. "Take his bloody head off!"

Julius turned and glared at Alexander again; the latter didn't flinch or show any sign of weakness.

"I've waited two thousand years for an experience like this," Julius spoke in a low growl. "You youngsters have no idea what it's like to walk this wretched earth for so long."

Alexander didn't dare to make a move or even respond, for fear of provoking Julius into further violence.

"Still, I suppose, time teaches you patience. Lucille's solution is agreeable to me, but know I won't wait forever." Julius addressed Alexander now. "If you don't deliver within a reasonable time frame, you may find me on your doorstep again. And at that time, there will be no mercy. If you can't deliver me the blood I want, I'll take an equal measure of yours."

Alexander never broke eye contact as long as Julius spoke. He took care not to show emotion: not fear, not relief at the proposed solution.

This would buy them time.

"The solution is agreeable," Alexander said.

"I don't believe it." Gillian threw her hands in the air and turned to leave.

Julius turned around and left the room within the blink of an eye. His guards followed, leaving behind only Lucille and Michael, who had remained at a safe distance throughout the entire confrontation.

"Thank you," Alexander said.

"I was only interpreting the rules, brother."

He smiled at her. Rules or otherwise, she'd taken the risk of opposing Julius, which was significant.

"Thank you anyway."

Lucille left as well, as did Michael, who would likely need to feed to heal his wounds. This meant only Alexander and Catherine remained.

"Whoa, that was intense," Catherine said, while reaching out for Alexander's arm.

He embraced her, held her tight. "I'm sorry you had to experience this."

Catherine's heart was still racing; Alexander could hear it clearly. He closed his eyes as he continued to hold her. Slowly but surely her body seemed to relax, bringing her heartbeat back under control. It occurred to him that although he still hadn't fed, her blood didn't call out to him with as much intensity as before. He could still smell it keenly, of course, but the ritual seemed to have dulled his thirst for now.

"Are you going to do it?" Catherine asked.

"Deliver him a Blood Bride?" Alexander said.

"Yes."

He remained quiet for a moment, while mulling it over. His aim first and foremost had been to keep Catherine safe. Now that they were bonded for life, her happiness would depend on his safety as well. In a way, he owed it to her to fulfill Julius' demand.

"I may not have much of a choice," he finally said.

Catherine didn't respond. She was still human, despite everything. The prospect of Alexander capturing and delivering some random woman to Julius would no doubt be horrifying to her.

Short of removing Julius as Principis of the Council, there was no other choice, though. And even then, he might no longer have the authority to officially punish Alexander, but he wouldn't hesitate to take matters into his own hands. The older vampires got, the more they felt they were above the law.

Alexander pulled back and looked into Catherine's captivating green eyes. He wouldn't have hesitated to kill Julius to protect her. But would he take such drastic action to protect a stranger?

The beginnings of tears started to collect in the corner of Catherine's eyes. Alexander ran the back of his finger across her cheek. He knew the right thing to do now.

"I'll do anything to keep you safe. And I'll do anything to make you happy. For now, Julius is off our backs, but once the time comes for him to collect his debt, I'll handle it however you want me to."

Catherine smiled through her tears. "I'm sorry. It's been a long day—night—whatever."

Alexander nodded. He repositioned his arms, one around her back and one along the bottom of her thighs, and lifted her up. She instinctively held on with both her arms around his neck and rested her head against his shoulder.

Just as they crossed the reception room and entrance, and started climbing the stairs, the old longcase clock on the upstairs landing started to strike one, two, three, four, five times.

Catherine must have been exhausted, after having been up the entire day as well as night. It would be a while before their schedules would align, so that their waking and sleeping times would coincide.

Alexander made his way through the hallway, straight to the master suite, and laid her down against the pillows.

"Not like this," she argued, suppressing a yawn.

Catherine gestured at him to sit with her, then rested her head in his lap and closed her eyes. He ran his hand through her silken hair until moments later, her breathing slowed and she drifted off into a peaceful slumber.

That was how they stayed, all morning, and well into the day. Their first day together as a wedded couple couldn't have started better. With Catherine resting and Alexander looking over her.

One major battle had passed; they'd won the right to live as man and wife. But Alexander had lived too long and seen too much to dare to predict the future beyond that. They'd figure out how to handle Julius and his unpaid debt in time.

First though, he'd guide Catherine on her way into this new life of hers. He caressed her hair again. Funny, how natural this felt, when actually, they barely knew one another. He couldn't wait to learn everything about her as she eased into it all.

"Did I fall asleep?" she mumbled groggily.

Alexander smiled. It wouldn't all be easy, especially for her at first, but he was convinced they'd find a way through.

Their bond was strong. And now they'd have forever to get to know each other.

EPILOGUE

So much had happened in these last two weeks, and for Cat, everything had changed.

She'd gone from a single, mostly carefree twenty-something right into a relationship so deep and committed, she couldn't imagine her life without it anymore. Alexander made her happy, like nobody ever had before.

But she hadn't just gained; she'd lost as well.

Her life in that little apartment in Shepherd's Bush with Shelly was over. She would never return there. Now, this huge mansion in the most desirable part of London was her home.

Similarly, that job she'd started—the internship at Sotheby's—had ended the moment she'd stepped into Alexander's house after her first auction.

She wouldn't work there anymore.

The next time she'd step into Sotheby's would be by Alexander's side, as a buyer. What would Ms. Pryce say to that?

In two short weeks, Cat felt like she'd changed so much. No longer the naive girl who fumbled over her words when an attractive man approached her—she had grown and matured.

Catherine sat down at the polished mahogany writing table in what was now her office and picked up a pen and a sheet of paper. This was her last job, before she could give herself fully to her new life.

As soon as she put the tip down on the first line, the words started to flow onto the page as if they had a mind of their own.

Dear Shelly,

Ever since our goodbye on the day I moved out, you'll have questions.

You'll probably wonder where I am, and whether I am safe. Rest assured, I am.

Everything is fine, and I am happy.

I couldn't tell you this at the time, for reasons that will become clear by the end of this letter. Remember I told you about that man, Alexander Broderick, who I met at the Halloween party? We are a couple now.

It all happened so fast, and yet I don't feel rushed at all. There isn't a doubt in my mind that everything has turned out exactly the way it should have.

Alexander's Blood Bride

Although I wish I could have spent more time with you, I am glad to be where I am now.

There are so many things I ought to explain to you, even if I have only just begun to understand them myself.

The supernatural is real, bizarre as it sounds. There are things out there that go beyond what modern science or even religion could explain.
Alexander is one of them, and in a way, now so am I.

This city, with its rich history and culture, has always been home to any number of creatures society at large doesn't know about. Sure, people used to tell stories, which over time have turned into myths, but most of us don't believe them. Now, I must say that I do. I can no longer assume that just because I haven't seen something in person, it doesn't exist.

One thing is absolutely certain though; vampires are real. There really are immortals out there who drink blood to survive. No, they don't kill; not anymore. They've even got a whole shadow government to make sure that they don't. They take great care to protect their secret, which is why I couldn't tell you all this so far.

Funny, isn't it? Two girls like us happened to walk into a Halloween party hosted by vampires? What's even funnier to me is that I am the one who has ended up here, surrounded by wealth and power. I never saw myself as strong, confident. The first time I walked into this house, I felt so out of place. Now it is starting to feel like home.

I have a man who adores me more than I could have dreamed of for myself. As much as I've given up to be with him, he risked more, including his own safety, to keep me safe. A small part of me still wonders if I'm worthy.

But every time he looks at me, his eyes tell me that I am.

One day, I hope you get something like this; perhaps not with a vampire, but with a regular guy.

It's the connection that counts. This is what love feels like. You deserve to find it too.

For now, this really is goodbye. Spending time together really isn't an option; you wouldn't be safe.

Alexander and I had to fight for the right to be together. Just knowing about this underworld of sorts is dangerous and there are people—other vampires—out there who are just waiting for us to slip up. As long as we follow the rules, we'll be safe, though.

When things calm down, maybe we will meet again, but I can't make any promises about the time frame. The truth is, now that I am part of this different world, the passing of time will take on a new meaning for me. It'll no longer be fleeting, but rather more steady and constant.

All I can do is hope, and wait for the right moment.

Live your life, be happy, find love.
All the best.

Love,

Your best friend, always, Cat

Cat put the pen down and stared at the now filled sheet of paper. One solitary tear threatened to escape her lid and roll down her cheek, but she caught it just in time with the back of her hand.

Then she took a deep breath, picked up the paper, folded it, and sealed it inside an envelope which already had Shelly's name written on the front.

This was it. The final goodbye.

Cat opened the drawer of her writing desk, and placed the envelope inside, on top of the one labeled "Mom."

Of course she'd never send these letters; that would put the people she loved, as well as herself, in grave danger. But it felt nice to be able to express everything she wanted to in writing. Just to get it off her chest.

She shut the drawer and with it, rid herself of any remaining melancholy. Then she got up and left the room. Down the stairs, through the entrance hall and reception, she had already learned the way through this house.

Inside the library, Alexander was already waiting for her in one of the old leather arm chairs.

"Done?" he asked.

She stood in front of him and smiled. "Yes, that was the last one."

"I wish you didn't have to do this, say goodbye to

everything you've known. But the letters really helped me when I was just turned."

Cat reached out for him and he immediately took her hand, tugging at it gently. She stepped up even closer to his chair and straddled him, wrapping her arms around his neck.

"Will that ever happen?" she asked.

Alexander circled her shoulder with his index finger. "What, whether you'll be turned?"

Cat nodded.

"There's no real need, as long as we're together. As long as I'm alive, you will be too. Our bond ensures it."

"I know, but still," Cat said.

Immortality no doubt came with its own host of downsides. She recalled the way he'd looked at the painting that hung above the bed in the master suite on their first meeting. This house on a sunny midsummer's day—that was something nocturnal beings would never get to see. Was it all worth it in the end?

Alexander shrugged. "If you want. Your wish is my command."

Cat didn't respond, not with words anyway. She leaned down and let her lips do the rest.

She knew he didn't want to change her; that her humanity was what had attracted him in the first place. She just loved to hear that he would, if she asked him to.

He responded eagerly to her kisses; his passion drew her in closer. His hand tightened around a fistful of her hair. She loved this harmony of gentle affection and intense passion that threatened to make him lose control.

"I love you," she whispered in his ear.

Alexander's body went tense and he got up, still carrying her in his arms. "I love you too," he growled, as he carried her up to the master suite within the blink of an eye, like only a vampire could. There, he showed her exactly how much.

These were still the early days of their relationship and who knew what the future might bring. But as long as she had his love, and he had hers, they would be fine.

***

ABOUT THE AUTHOR

Dear Reader,

Thanks for reading Alexander's Blood Bride. Although at the time I'm writing this it's not even a year since I released my debut series, Scottish Werebears, I'm not new to writing in general. In fact, my mom still tells me to this day about how I would make up stories, and attempt to record them in my clumsy, shaky handwriting from the moment I learned to read and write. From there I went on to write fan fiction and other stuff meant for my own eyes only.

I've always enjoyed stories of the paranormal. Vampires, shape shifters, witches and magic, all featured in the books I loved the most, even when I was still growing up. But it wasn't until much later that I got into romance. One of the first writers (a self published author just like me!) I came across was Tina Folsom, via her Scanguards Vampire series. I was hooked. From there I went on to read more paranormal romance until I found a new kind of hero I loved: bear shifters, like the kind written by Milly Taiden, Zoe Chant, and T.S. Joyce. What I love about bears is how they can be all strong and independent, a bit reclusive, and almost grumpy, but they always end up having a heart of gold (plus they tend to know their food, and we all know that a man who can cook is doubly sexy). All that (except for the shifting into a powerful bear) almost exactly describes the sort of man I ended up falling for and marrying in real life, so it's no surprise that this is what I started my publishing career with.

But no matter how many bear shifter books I've written, I've always longed to write a Vampire romance. Finally, once the Scottish Werebears series was complete, it was time to fulfill this dream. I'm really pleased with how it's turned out; it has everything I look for in vampire books. A dangerous attraction between the hero and heroine which could end in tragedy, a bunch of rival vampires wanting the heroine for themselves, making the hero choose sides. And an ending that shows that even if you're seemingly incompatible (one of them is constantly battling the urge to kill the other; how much worse can it get?), you can still find happiness.

To find out more, check:

LoreleiMoone.com (And why not sign up for the newsletter to be the first to find out about new releases.)

You can also get in touch with me via Facebook (search for Lorelei Moone), or email at info@loreleimoone.com

x Lorelei